JACK

IN THE

GREEN

by DIANE CAPRI

Published by: AugustBooks
http://www.AugustBooks.com

ISBN-13: 978-1-940768-30-4

Original cover design by Cory Clubb
Interior layout by Author E.M

Jack in the Green is a work of fiction. Names, characters, places, and incidents either are the product of the author's imagination or are used fictitiously, and any resemblance to actual persons, living or dead, business establishments, events, or locales is entirely coincidental.

Published in the United States of America.

Visit the author's website:
http://www.DianeCapri.com

ALSO BY DIANE CAPRI

The Hunt for Justice Series
Due Justice
Twisted Justice
Secret Justice
Wasted Justice
Raw Justice
Mistaken Justice
Cold Justice
Fatal Distraction
Fatal Enemy

The Hunt for Jack Reacher Series:
Don't Know Jack
Jack in a Box
Jack and Kill
Get Back Jack
Jack in the Green

JACK

IN THE

GREEN

Thank you to some of the best readers in the world: Natalie Chernow, Angie Shaw (Noah Daniel), Dan Chillman (Danimal), Lynette Bartos (Derek Bartos), Teresa Burgess (Trista Blanke) for participating in our character naming giveaways which make this book a bit more personal and fun for all of us.

Perpetually, to Lee Child, with unrelenting gratitude.

CAST OF PRIMARY CHARACTERS

Kim L. Otto
Carlos M. Gaspar

Thomas Weston
Samantha Weston
Steven Kent

Jessica Kimball
Jennifer Lane
Willa Carson

Charles Cooper
Jacqueline Roscoe

and
Jack Reacher

CHAPTER ONE

FBI SPECIAL AGENT CARLOS Gaspar lounged back in the driver's seat of the rental sedan to stretch his bad right leg, but all senses remained fully alert. The last time he'd been on MacDill Air Force Base, Gaspar's partner had been wounded and a man had died resisting routine arrest. It was his sixth sense that rankled. He had a bad feeling about the place. He couldn't shake it.

He'd chosen the center lane and pulled into place behind a line passing steadily through the guard stations. One SUV ahead now, sporting a patriotic car magnet.

Veteran, probably.

Once upon a time, a veteran could be trusted to follow protocol. Veterans knew the rules. Knew they couldn't bring personal weapons on the base or enter restricted areas. They didn't need to be watched. But increasingly, veterans and even active military seemed to be going off the rails now and then.

Sometimes for good cause.

Reacher was a veteran. Gaspar never allowed himself to forget that.

He preferred the smaller Bayshore Gate entrance. Closer to their destination. Less traffic. Only one lane. Only one sentry. Ruled out for just that reason: Because that sentry had fewer vehicles to inspect, she'd be more likely to ask thorough questions Gaspar would not answer. Which would probably land him in the brig and he didn't have time for that today.

The main gate entrance to Tampa's MacDill Air Force Base was less treacherous because he could get lucky. Three traffic lanes fed into the main gate. Each lane supported two security stations configured to more closely resemble drive-through windows at a prosperous suburban bank than a military checkpoint.

Except bank tellers don't wear BDUs and side arms.

Base security handled 20,000 people passing

through every day as a matter of routine. Today was not routine. Which meant security would be relaxed, maybe.

From behind aviator sunglasses, Gaspar watched the security process unfold predictably around him. But the whole setup of the event felt wrong. Too much lead time since the target's attendance was announced, for one thing. Too public. Too many people. An unpredictable target with too many enemies and too many secrets.

And the usual dearth of good Intel about everything.

It was a bad combination and he didn't like it, even without factoring Reacher into the equation.

Not that it mattered to the Boss what Gaspar liked or didn't like.

The flashing sign outside the security checkpoint declared Force Protection Condition Alpha, meaning only slightly elevated security in place. Probably bumped up a notch because of expected increased civilian attendance at the annual memorial service honoring deceased members of military families, he figured. He took that as a good omen. The base commander couldn't feel as uneasy as Gaspar did or security would be tighter.

He palmed his plastic VA card and flipped it

through his fingers like a Las Vegas card shark, then tapped it rapidly on the steering wheel as if that would encourage the security personnel to speedier service. The Boss said Gaspar's VA card would serve as required military ID to enter the base because of the hundreds of people expected at the memorial ceremony. Gaspar figured the Boss had greased the wheels to make it so, as he usually did.

Gaspar glanced over at his current partner to confirm that she wasn't freaking out any more than usual. "How late are we?"

He'd bought the aviators months ago to block the blinding glare of Miami sunlight. Now, they also served to shield him from her penetrating evaluation of his every move.

His shades weren't needed at the moment, as it happened. "Twenty-five minutes," FBI Special Agent Kim Otto replied, without lifting her gaze from her smart phone's screen.

He'd found Otto's nuanced perception almost telepathic in the weeks since the Boss had paired them up for reasons unknown. They worked well together. He liked her. She seemed to like him well enough. The partnership was improving.

But he was still wary.

Otto's self-preservation instincts never relaxed. Not for half a moment. Ever.

He had a family to support. And twenty years to go. And this was the only field assignment he'd been offered since his disabling injury. Playing second on the team to a woman ten years greener added to the insult. Yet he felt grateful to have the work, mainly because it was the only option he had.

But the Reacher job was more dangerous than they'd been told. Much more. As a result, Otto was jumpier than a mosquito on steroids. She would replace him in a hot second if she became the slightest bit concerned about his reliability.

And she'd be smart to cut him out. He'd do the same to her if their roles were reversed. Maybe even as their roles were now.

So he had to be careful. Safer that way.

Which meant he needed as much distance as he could summon inside the sedan before she sensed any danger.

Why was it so hot in here? He flipped up the fan speed on the air conditioning.

The security staffer took three steps back from the SUV in front of them and the vehicle passed through. Gaspar raised his foot off the brake and allowed the sedan to roll forward until his window was even with the security officer.

Gaspar's window remained closed, following the Boss's explicit instructions.

He held up his photo VA card between his left index and middle fingers, almost like a salute. The card had a bar code on it. If the security guard followed procedure, she'd scan the card. He waited. She did, and waved him through without hassle. The scan was routine. The data should get lost in the mountain of data collected every day. As long as Gaspar did nothing to draw attention to himself, his presence here today should remain undiscovered by the wrong people. He hoped.

He let the sedan roll on through the checkpoint, releasing a breath he hadn't known he'd been holding. If they'd been required to offer FBI badges or answer questions, or if security had searched the sedan, everything would have become a lot more complicated. His life was already complicated enough.

As much as they relied upon the Boss's promise of lax security in their case, he felt Otto's disapproval emitting like sonar waves. How many other VA cards had been waved through today? Was Reacher's one of them? And who checked the civilians required only to show their drivers' licenses for this special event?

But they'd passed the first hurdle. They were on base. Unidentified. So far, so good.

CHAPTER TWO

THE BOSS HAD SAID their movements would be unrestricted inside the gate. Except for certain areas where armed guards were posted. It would be easy enough to avoid those.

"Notice anything worrisome since you were here last?" Otto asked.

He glanced her way. She had her head turned to look out her window, scanning for threats, probably. Especially from behind, she looked like a tiny Asian doll. The top of her deceptively fragile-looking shoulder rested well below the bottom edge of the big sedan's window. If she hadn't put that alligator clamp on her seatbelt at the retractor, it could have sliced her head off her neck in an accident.

"Well?" she said, more insistent this time,

scanning through the front windshield now. When he still didn't reply, she glanced his way.

He shrugged, combed his hair with splayed fingers, turned his head and made a show of looking around.

MacDill Air Force Base was both a country club for military families and a war zone. A strange combination of all-inclusive resort and weaponized death star. It boasted a beach and golf course and a full-featured campground for veterans dubbed "Famcamp," where his last trip here had ended in disaster. Inside the buildings you'd find standard Government Issue everything.

Then there were the heavily armed guards protecting the strategic commands that earned the base its lofty importance to national defense and control over state-of-the-art killing machines around the world.

Before his injury, Gaspar brought his kids to the annual MacDill AirFest. He'd been here on special assignments while he was in the army, and once or twice since he'd been assigned to the FBI's Miami Field Office. He hoped today's arrest would go more smoothly than his last one here.

"It's a simple question, Chico," Otto said, continuing her recon.

"Wish I had a simple answer." He took in the view through the glass again—right, left, front and in the rear view mirror—seeking any unfamiliar additions to the geography.

The base consumed every inch of the small peninsula jutting out into Tampa Bay. The last time he'd been here it was to attend a retirement dinner in the officers' club, which had since been demolished. Nothing abnormal in that. When new facilities were required, it generally meant old stuff was demolished and replaced.

Today's event was a perfect example. Hundreds of civilians were expected at a temporary outdoor stage like it had always been there. The chosen site was close to the Strategic Operations Command Memorial Wall honoring the fallen. Nearby, multiple command centers for war. Death and life combined in paradise, to jarring effect.

"What time is Weston scheduled to be arrested?" he asked.

"After the service," she said, checking her Seiko. "Maybe three hours from now. Plenty of time to get what we came for and get out before the arresting agents move."

"Plenty of time for all sorts of things to

happen." He shrugged as if unconcerned, but figured she knew better.

Building a current file on Jack Reacher—filling in the blanks after he'd left the Army's 110th Special Investigations Unit—had seemed routine initially. Until they read the background file, which was thin. Too thin. Since, they'd been pulling the scabs off old wounds Reacher had caused. It meant infiltrating enemy territory every time. Both Gaspar and Otto had fresh scars to prove it.

No reason to believe Weston would be an easier interview subject than the others had been. In fact, from what they'd learned about the man, there was every reason to believe he'd be worse.

They'd been warned to watch out for Reacher, who came, destroyed and departed like a liger. Neither he nor Otto needed to be reminded to watch for him, but Gaspar wanted to believe it unlikely Reacher would try to get Weston today. Their feud was sixteen years old and surely even Reacher might have lost track of Weston in all that time.

"Weston has stayed out of Reacher's way all this time," Otto said. "So why is Weston sticking his neck out by attending this particular memorial ceremony? He could have come any time. The base holds these generic memorials for military family members to pay their respects every year. Weston contacted them a month ago and said he wanted to attend this particular service. It doesn't make any sense, does it?"

"Not to me," Gaspar replied. "So we do what we do."

"Meaning what?"

"Meaning we stay alert. We're missing something important, Sunshine."

Her tone was hard in reply. "So what else is new?"

Gaspar parked the sedan an assured clear distance from civilian traffic around the memorial site, which seemed to have a disproportionate number of handicapped parking spaces, and they stepped out into the warm November sunshine.

Gaspar stretched like a lizard. After the past few weeks in frigid cold, he'd forgotten how good Florida sunshine could feel a few days before Thanksgiving.

Otto watched him from just over the hood of the sedan, but said nothing.

When he stepped around the car, they began walking toward the memorial site, keeping a few yards' distance from other early arrivals. Some were in wheelchairs. Some moved jerkily on new prosthetic limbs. One mystery solved: the excess of handicapped spaces. The memorial service was an annual event to honor fallen members of military families. Many attendees were wounded veterans themselves.

Gaspar's limp was pronounced at first, but eased with exercise, as it usually did.

"I know you're running through it again in your head," Gaspar said with a grin to distract her from his limping. "Just verbalize for me while you're at it. Another run-through never hurts."

She scowled as if he'd falsely accused her. He hadn't. She never stopped thinking, analyzing, crunching data in her head, even if it was the same data, over and over. He didn't complain. Her odd habits had already saved his ass more than once.

"The subject is retired Army Lieut. Col. Alfred Weston." She rattled off the few important facts they'd received in the Boss's materials: "Sixteen-plus years ago, Weston was posted here on a classified assignment. No details in the file. Weston's wife and three children were murdered. Reacher somehow became the lead Army investigator on the case. He thought Weston was the killer."

"Why?"

"Who knows?" she said, as if she was slightly irritated at Reacher's unfathomable behavior. Which she probably was.

"But Reacher couldn't prove Weston did it," Gaspar continued for her, "and it turned out the real shooter was arrested quickly by the locals." He fingered the Tylenol in his pocket. He'd swallow another one when she wasn't watching. His doctors prescribed narcotic pain medication, but he couldn't risk taking it. Tylenol was the strongest thing he'd allow himself while they were working.

She said, "After the killer's arrest, the official investigation of Weston ended."

"Unofficially, Reacher wouldn't let it go," Gaspar went on. Reacher never let anything go once he had his teeth into it. Otto was the same way. For sheer bulldog tenacity, Reacher and Otto were as alike as bookends.

"Weston's been living abroad," Otto said, "Middle East mostly, since he left the Army under a cloud of Reacher's making." She stopped talking abruptly, as if she didn't want to mention the rest.

Gaspar's right leg was feeling stronger. The cramping easing. Limp nearly under control. Pain ever-present, sure, but he could handle pain. He'd been handling it a good long while.

"And now," Otto said, "Weston's accused of major crimes against the U.S. Government. Various forms of corruption, mostly, related to the private security company he operates. A few allegations of using unauthorized force and excessive force. Suspected manslaughter of civilians is at the center of it. A lot of conflicting evidence. Nothing actually proved so far, but plenty to support an arrest and interrogation." She hesitated half a breath. "This is the first time Weston's been on American soil in the past sixteen years."

Same facts he'd memorized on the plane. He hadn't missed anything. He still didn't like it.

Gaspar mulled for a couple more steps before he asked, "Why come back at all? He's got nothing here. Why not just stay offshore and make Uncle Sam send covert operations after him if we wanted him badly enough?"

She shrugged as if the answer didn't matter, when Gaspar knew it did.

"Once they snatch him," she said, "he'll be locked up and off limits to us. We need to get to him today." She took another breath and glanced again at the plain Seiko on her narrow wrist. "We've got less than an hour before the service starts."

Gaspar felt his eyebrows knitting together. Their mission still wouldn't make sense. "Why should Weston tell us anything useful?"

"The Boss says Weston blames Reacher for his troubles and wants to even the score. We're supposed to give Weston that chance and strongly encourage him to take it." Unconsciously, perhaps, she patted her gun under her blazer.

"We're striking out with Reacher's friends so we'll squeeze his enemies instead?" A harsh, dry chuckle escaped Gaspar's lips. "Sounds a little like sticking your head in the mouth of a hungry carnivore doesn't it?"

Otto said nothing.

CHAPTER THREE

THEY'D BEEN ALLOTTED ONE hour to get in, get what they could, and get out without crossing paths with the arresting agents or stepping in another pile of stink from unknown origins. Flight and traffic delays had sucked up more than half of their time already.

"Your gun's loaded, right?" she said, patting hers again as if she didn't realize she'd touched it.

"Come on, Sunshine." He ran both hands through his hair again and stuffed them in his trouser pockets. "We've been over this. We can't discharge weapons we're illegally carrying. Do you have any idea what would happen if we did that?"

"I'm familiar with procedures," she snapped.

"And you're familiar with prison sentences, too."

She seemed unimpressed with his reasoning. "Weston's made enemies here and around the world. A few have a strong appetite for vengeance."

Gaspar knew she was worrying about one particular enemy. So was he.

"Unlikely Reacher knows Weston's here," he said. "How would he have heard? The man's far enough off the grid even the Boss can't find him. Not likely anyone else can."

Finding Reacher wasn't the issue, though. The question was whether Reacher would find Weston. Or them—a growing possibility, the longer they went looking for him. Reacher had friends. By now, smart money said at least one of those friends had somehow passed along that they were on his trail.

"Reacher lives to piss on the other guy's grave," Otto said. "He's a highly qualified sniper. The only non-Marine to win the 1000-yard invitational rifle competition."

"It would be crazy to try to kill Weston here where he'll be so heavily guarded. A good sniper would choose a highway location. Shoot from a vehicle. Make a clean getaway," Gaspar said.

Again her hand passed over the lump in her blazer. "I'm saying we need a Plan B. Guns work for me. Unless you've got a better plan."

He didn't.

They'd arrived at the ceremony site. Setup was completed and the audience was slowly filing in. Gaspar estimated seating for about 1,000 people. A temporary, elevated stage at the front, a center podium flanked by four chairs on either side. He saw flat, open parking lots behind the stage where official vehicles and emergency personnel waited. A dark sedan pulled in from the opposite side of the parking lot. Which meant there was a second means of ingress and egress to the area.

One more entrance or escape route to cover. Not ideal.

He studied the site's perimeter. Otto was right. Weston's tenure here at MacDill, and with the Army in general, had produced more enemies than most men accumulated in a lifetime. Yet, today Weston would stand in an open field on an elevated stage surrounded by too many spots for a moderately good shooter to hide.

It felt foolhardy to Gaspar. Weston had to feel the same way.

Any military man would.

Which was one of the things that made the setup feel so profoundly wrong.

Gaspar identified the most likely shelter points for snipers within a seventy yard range. Any military sniper was reliable at five times that distance. There were several good ones and a few more that a sniper as good as Reacher could use to kill and disappear before anyone found his nest. What they had learned about Reacher was that even though he could kill from a distance at any time, he preferred to handle his problems up close and personal. Gaspar had felt like prey every day since he'd received the Reacher assignment. The only reasonable solution was to ignore it and press on.

The base held plenty of weapons and ammo and legitimate personnel who were trained to use them. In theory, all arms were accounted for and all non-security personnel were prohibited from possessing personal weapons on base. In theory.

Like most theories, that one was obviously unreliable. Gaspar knew for sure that at least two people carrying unauthorized weapons were standing in this precise spot already. Seemed to him more than likely there'd be others.

"You know what worries me?" Otto asked.

He laughed. "Everything worries you, Sunshine."

She glared at him. "Why did Weston agree to attend this ceremony, make himself an easy target?"

"I was just wondering that myself," Gaspar said. "Maybe he's got a death wish."

"Or homicidal intent," she said.

Gaspar didn't argue. Either option was possible.

He again checked the potential sniper points he could identify and pointed them out to her. Shooting into a crowd and hitting only the intended target was not a simple thing, but it wasn't impossible, either. The best locations were in the west, with the sun behind him. Firing out of the sun was every sniper's basic preference.

"Just stay out of the line of fire," he told her. "If my partner is shot and killed on a military base, I'll be buried in paperwork for the rest of my natural lifetime. I've got kids to raise."

"Your concern is touching," she said, just before she slugged him in the bicep hard enough to knock him off balance. He righted himself and hammed it up a little to conceal how easily she could fell him.

"Enough horsing around. Be serious for the next ninety minutes, will you?" she scolded.

She was tiny, but fierce. He admired that about her.

Not that he'd let her know it.

Movement near the stage caught his attention. "There's Weston. Let's go."

He set off toward the opposite side of the venue at a good clip. Otto struggled to keep pace at first and then strode past him until it was his turn to struggle. They closed the distance to the edge of the stage where Weston stood at ground level, flanked by a military escort and two women. The escort would be Corporal Noah Daniel, according to the Boss's instructions.

Twenty feet behind Weston stood three bulky civilians wearing navy business suits, white shirts and rep ties, and thick-soled shoes. These could only be private bodyguards. More holes in the "no guns on base" theory, Gaspar figured.

He slowed so Otto reached their target first, allowing Gaspar time to gather quick impressions of the Weston group.

The older woman was Samantha Weston. She was draped in ridiculous fashion garments that probably came from Paris or Milan without benefit of filtering through American good sense.

She was fortyish. Lanky. Lean. Artfully styled hair. Handsomely well-constructed.

Gaspar could spot skilled plastic surgery and *haute couture* across a dim and crowded Miami ballroom. No detective work required here, though. Mrs. Weston's familiarity with both was revealed by Tampa's brutally honest sunlight.

The younger woman standing slightly behind Mrs. Weston was well groomed but plain. Wholesome. Smallish. About thirty, or a couple of years either side, Gaspar guessed. Dark hair. Short, scrubbed fingernails. Everything about her appearance was professionally no-nonsense.

And something else.

She seemed familiar.

A certain lilt to her nose, crinkles around her eyes as she squinted into the sun, dimple in her chin.

Who was she?

Wife of an acquaintance? Ring-less fingers ruled out that option.

Maybe she resembled a celebrity or even a crime victim from a prior case.

He waited a moment for the information to bubble up. No luck. He couldn't place her.

Next, from behind the aviators he scanned the

subject like a full body x-ray machine. Weston's dark suit covered him from turkey neck to shiny, cap-toed shoes. All visible body parts were pathetic. Gaspar's scan noted pasty skin, eye pouches, jowls, tremors. Weston was fifty-five, maybe? But he looked every moment of twenty years older.

The expat life in Iraq as a military contractor suspected of murdering local civilians carried its own unhealthy burdens, sure. In Weston's case, the added pressure of surviving the murder of his wife and children on U.S. soil couldn't be easy. Guilt might have gnawed his organs, maybe. Whatever the cause, he looked like he was being eaten alive.

Otto presented herself to them. "Corporal Daniel. Colonel Weston. Mrs. Weston." She hesitated briefly before reaching out to the unidentified younger woman.

"Jennifer Lane," the woman said, extending her hand for a firm shake with Otto first, then Gaspar. "I'm Mrs. Weston's lawyer."

Instantly, Samantha Weston became more concerning. In Gaspar's experience, only people already in trouble and expecting worse trouble traveled with a lawyer.

"I am FBI Special Agent Kim Otto and this is my partner Special Agent Carlos Gaspar. We'd like to talk to Colonel Weston for a few minutes, if you don't mind."

The expression settling on Weston's face was something close to satisfaction. He didn't smile, exactly. More like a smirk. So Weston had expected them. Or someone like them. Which made Gaspar more uneasy than he already was. Why would Weston anticipate that cops would approach him today? The Boss said Weston's arrest was a sting. Gaspar could dream up a dozen explanations, but none of them were good news.

Corporal Daniel performed as ordered. "Mrs. Weston, Ms. Lane, our base chaplain would like a word with you before we begin," he said, leading Samantha Weston away by a firm forearm grip.

Attorney Jennifer Lane followed her client like a pit bull on a leash.

Gaspar positioned himself facing Weston, better to observe and avoid the sniper positions he'd previously noted. Otto stood to one side, also out of identifiable firing lines. Weston remained an easy target and had to know it, but didn't seem to care.

"Sir, we'll only take a few moments of your time," Otto said. "We're hoping you can help us with some background data about the investigating military police officer on your wife's murder case."

"Reacher," Weston said, as though naming an enemy more heinous than Bin Laden. Then, eagerly, "Is he with you?"

Otto's expression, betraying equal parts horror and astonishment at the very thought, was quickly squelched.

Gaspar hid his grin behind a cough. One mystery solved. Weston meant to lure Reacher here today.

And maybe he had. Gaspar didn't find that option comforting in the least.

"We haven't seen him recently," Gaspar said, truthfully enough. He slouched a little and settled his hands into his trouser pockets because it made him seem friendlier. Gaspar knew many successful interrogation techniques, but none of them worked unless the subject wanted to talk. Most of the problem was making them want to. Once they wanted to tell him everything, witnesses were nearly impossible to shut up.

Disappointed that they hadn't served up his quarry, Weston became more suspicious. "Why are you collecting background on Reacher?"

The half-truth rolled more easily off Otto's tongue after weeks of practice, "We're completing a routine investigation."

"Why?"

"He's being considered for a special assignment."

"Cannon fodder? Road kill?" Weston's sharp retorts came fast. "Those are the only jobs Reacher's fit for."

"Meaning what?" Otto asked, unintimidated.

Weston said, "My wife and children were executed. By cowards. While I was serving my country."

"Nothing to do with Reacher, right?" Otto asked.

Weston's face reddened and his eyes narrowed. "Reacher accused me. He arrested me. I wasn't there to see my children buried. I wasn't there to see my wife buried. I sat in a jail cell instead." He clenched and unclenched his fists at his side. "This is the first memorial service I've ever been able to attend for my slain family. You call that nothing? I sure as hell don't."

"Not unreasonable of Reacher, though," Otto said, detached, cool. "Most people are murdered by someone close to them. Anybody who watches television knows that. Reacher wasn't out of line when he considered you a prime suspect."

Weston's chest heaved. He shifted his slight

weight and leaned closer to Otto, towering unsteadily over her. She didn't flinch. She remained the polar opposite of cowed. Gaspar figured Weston wasn't used to having any woman stand her ground with him, much less one nearly half his size.

Weston lowered his voice to a mighty pianissimo and still Otto didn't budge even half an inch. "When Reacher found out he was wrong about me? What did he do?"

Otto lifted her shoulders and opened her palms, unimpressed. "I give up."

Otto's behavior enraged Weston a bit more. He leaned in and all but engulfed her like a vulture's shadow. She didn't move and said nothing.

Then, as if he'd flipped some sort of internal switch, he released the stranglehold on his fists and relaxed his posture. Regular breathing resumed. Sweat beads on his forehead and above his upper lip glistened in the sunlight. A breeze had kicked up, carrying floral scents from the tropical plants in and around the base. A breeze that any good sniper could easily accommodate.

When Weston spoke again, he sounded almost civil, as if Otto had asked him about nothing more personal than last night's dinner menu.

The guy was a sociopath, Gaspar thought.

Clearly. Total nut-job. All the signs were there. He'd seen it too many times before.

"It's unfortunate that Reacher's still alive. If I see him before you do, he won't be. Please tell him that for me." His tone reflected the controlled calm Gaspar recognized as subdued rage. A hallmark of stone cold killers, crazy or not.

Gaspar asked, "Why did Reacher think you killed your family? We haven't seen the whole file. Was there some evidence against you?"

"Ask him next time you see him." Weston folded his hands in front of his scrawny abdomen, miming that he had all the patience in the world to do nothing but humor them.

"Right now I'm asking you."

Attendees had been filing in steadily as they talked and now filled the chairs in the audience as well as on the stage. Again, Gaspar noticed a significant number of disabled men and women. Many of them were young. Too young.

Not much time left.

Weston's satisfied smirk turned up a notch. "You work for Cooper, don't you?"

Hearing him utter the Boss's name was a sharp jab, but Gaspar recognized a classic deflection and refused the bait. Whatever happened after Reacher left the Army, he'd been a good cop. After twenty minutes with Weston, Gaspar was ready to believe anything Reacher reported about Weston on Reacher's word alone.

"Why did Reacher think you'd killed your own family?" Gaspar asked again.

Weston said nothing.

Otto stepped in. "Have you communicated with Reacher since you left the army, Colonel?"

"I've been living abroad."

Otto said, "The globe is a lot smaller than it used to be. People travel."

"Too bad Reacher hasn't been to Iraq." And like that, Weston's control again seemed to snap. "I'd happily kill the bastard. Cooper, too, given the chance."

"What's your beef with the Boss?" Gaspar asked. The guy was crazy, but whatever he thought about the Boss, it was better to find out than get caught napping.

"We all wore the green back then. We were brothers in arms. We were supposed to be taking care of each other. The Army's family, man," Weston said. "You served, didn't you? You've got the bearing. I can smell the green on you. You've gotta know what I mean."

Gaspar did know. He was tempted to make a sarcastic remark about simply surviving being a better outcome than what had happened to Weston's real family. Not to mention the dead and disabled who served under Weston's command. But instead Gaspar said, "Right."

Weston stopped a second to wipe the spittle from the corner of his mouth, to gather himself. When he spoke again, the switch had again been tripped. The controlled calm had returned. "You really don't know, do you?"

"Know what?" Otto asked.

"You can't be that stupid." Weston's lip curled up. The kind of smirk that made Gaspar want to break his face. "Cooper's the biggest snake alive. Always has been. Turn your back and he'll bite you in the ass. Reacher was Cooper's go-to guy. The two of them were behind everything that happened to me."

Gaspar shook his head exaggeratedly, like he'd heard better tales from the Brothers Grimm. "You think Reacher killed your family? On Cooper's orders? Then blamed you?"

"I've had a lot of years to think this through. Cooper and Reacher had a vendetta going against me. It had to be them." He paused, smiling like a demented circus clown. "That's the only possible answer."

Otto intervened. "The hit man said you hired him. He testified you wanted your family killed."

Once again, Weston's agitation resurfaced. The man was like a carnival ride. His face reddened. His eyes narrowed. His lips pressed hard together and he stuck out his chin. "Lies!" he shouted, loud enough for members of the crowd filtering in nearby to hear and turn to stare.

"Close enough for government work," Otto replied without flinching. "You'd been threatened by the gang you tried to rip off. You were told what would happen to your family. You failed to deliver their money. Reacher had nothing to do with any of that."

She didn't mention the Boss had reached out by sending them here today and probably by sending Reacher back then, too. Gaspar wasn't the only one who noticed.

Weston rocked closer and loomed over Otto again. "Little girl, if you were half as smart as you think you are, you'd have stopped believing Cooper's fairy tales long ago." He lifted balled fists and unclenched his hands, reaching toward her. He looked like he wanted to shake her by her slender neck until she stopped breathing.

Gaspar hoped he'd try. Otto would knock Weston on his ass the second he touched her. But all this talk about Reacher had heightened his tension, too. On the way through security, Gaspar had been concerned. Now, he felt wired tight, ready to snap.

Before Weston had a chance to complete his move, Samantha Weston appeared by her husband's side like a defending Valkyrie from nowhere.

When Weston didn't back down, his wife placed a firm hand on his shoulder. "Tom, darling. It's time."

Otto had yet to move so much as an eyelash. She said in her normal voice, "We'll finish our questions after the service, Colonel."

Weston didn't flinch for another full second. Then he shook off his wife's hand, turned, marched toward the stage, climbed the steps and stood, waiting for Samantha to catch up.

Gaspar and Otto watched in silence until both Westons reached their positions on the stage with the other honorees of the day's service, and then continued to watch them.

The breeze had whipped up to gusty bursts.

Unpredictable. Which would make a sniper's job harder. Not impossible. Some would consider the wind a worthy challenge. Reacher was probably one of them.

Eyes still forward, Gaspar said, "I'm okay with staying a while. We've got a few hours before our flight. But what do you think he'll say later that he wouldn't say now?"

"Weston's the first person we've met who is willing to tell us anything at all about Reacher. I'm not leaving until I hear every last word I can wring out of him." After a full second or so, she asked, "You think the Boss sent us here to see if Weston could actually pin anything on him and Reacher?"

"I gave up trying to guess the Boss's motives years ago." Gaspar nodded in the direction of the entrance, where two males dressed in FBI-normal stood to one side. "More importantly, what are you planning to tell those guys when they ask who we are and what the hell we're doing here?"

"You'll think of something," she replied, focused now on the tableau playing out on the stage. "Who is that reporter talking to Weston?"

CHAPTER FOUR

THE REPORTER WORE A press pass on a chain around her neck, a video camera slung over her back and a recorder of some sort raised to capture a conversation Gaspar couldn't hear. Weston and his wife spoke with her briefly before the lawyer stepped in and stopped the inquiry. A short verbal exchange between the reporter and Lane, the lawyer, ended when Lane herded the Westons to their seats.

Gaspar wondered again where he had seen that lawyer before. He couldn't place her, but he knew her. He was sure of it.

The reporter raised her camera and snapped a few photos of the entire scene before she walked down the four steps from the stage and onto the path directly toward Otto and Gaspar. When she was close enough, he read her press pass.

Jess Kimball, *Taboo Magazine*.

Odd that *Taboo* would be covering Weston. *Taboo* was in the vein of *Vanity Fair*, its only real competitor. Gaspar had seen both magazines around the house because his wife subscribed. Both covered popular culture, fashion, and current affairs. *Taboo* was newer, a bit edgier, maybe, but covered the same beat. Retired military officers were neither of the national glossies' usual subject or audience. Which made Gaspar more curious instead of less.

Gaspar stepped in front of the reporter before she walked past. "Ms. Kimball, a moment of your time?"

Her eyes, when she focused on his, were piercingly blue. Nostrils flared. "Yes?"

"Why is *Taboo Magazine* interested in Colonel Weston?"

"And you are?" Kimball held the last word in a long, hostile invitation to reply.

"Carlos Gaspar. FBI. This is my partner, Kim Otto."

Kimball considered something for a moment before she answered. "Sorry to say, I'm no threat to Weston."

"What's your interest?" Gaspar asked again.

"My mission is to make sure victims get justice. Especially children."

"What does that mean?" Otto asked.

"Ever heard of Dominick Dunne?"

"The *Vanity Fair* reporter who covered all those infamous trials after his daughter was murdered," Otto replied.

"I covered Weston's case a while ago when the gunman who killed Weston's family was executed by the State of Florida. Weston was living in Iraq at the time. No chance to wrap up with him until now without traveling to a war zone."

Otto asked, "Why did you say 'the gunman'?"

"He pulled the trigger. But he wasn't the reason those kids and their mom were murdered. We've got Colonel Weston to thank for that," Kimball said, in the same way she'd have thanked Typhoid Mary for robust health.

"Weston denies involvement," Otto said, "and no connection was established."

The ceremony was opened by a chaplain, who began with an invocation. Those in the audience with the physical ability stood and bowed their heads. Many closed their eyes. Immediate, eerie quiet reigned.

Kimball whispered. "The Army's cop got it right at the outset."

"Reacher?"

A woman nearby raised her head and glared toward them. Otto held her remaining questions until the brief invocation concluded and the audience returned as one to their seats.

Normal squirming set a low, baseline volume beneath which Kimball replied. "Weston's family was murdered because of Weston. He's got their blood on his hands. Doesn't matter who pulled the trigger and killed them in their beds."

"You're the reason the Westons brought a lawyer here today, huh?" Gaspar asked.

Kimball shook her head with a sour smile. "More likely the divorce Samantha's lawyer filed yesterday the second they set foot on U.S. soil," she said. "Either way, the Westons have more than me to be worried about."

"Why do you say that?" Otto asked.

"You wouldn't be here without an agenda." Kimball tilted her head toward the entrance where the two agents waited. "More of your tribe over there. I'm guessing it's not an FBI picnic. Weston's about to get his. Finally. You can be sure I'm here to get photos."

Silence settled over the crowd again, except for a few members who were quietly crying. Occasionally, a brain-injured veteran would speak inappropriately. There were too many brain-injured veterans after the long war. They'd become a part of normal civilian life for military families. Another burden for the stalwart to bear with dignity. Everyone ignored the interruptions.

Still at the side of the stage, Otto, Gaspar, and Kimball were the only people standing. Drawing too much of the wrong attention.

Kimball handed Gaspar her card.

"Call me later. I'll fill you in," she whispered and slipped away to join the other reporters seated near the opposite side of the stage. She was well within her equipment's visual and audio range and beyond the reach of FBI interrogation while the memorial service continued.

CHAPTER FIVE

THE AUDIENCE HAD EXPANDED while Gaspar had been preoccupied by Weston and then Kimball. Seating was now filled to capacity and additional attendees stood blocking the aisles and the exits. His sightline to the official vehicles behind the stage was obscured, but he could see enough to confirm they remained in place. He couldn't see whether Weston's limo and bodyguards were still present, but they probably were.

On the stage, all the chairs were occupied now. Both Westons and the chaplain were seated to the right of the podium. The base commander wasn't present, but the resident Army Military Intelligence unit was represented by a one-star Brigadier General Gaspar didn't know seated to the left of the podium with two civilians. Enlarged photos of the individuals—and, in Weston's case, the family—being remembered today rested on easels blocking Gaspar's sightline to the area behind the seated dignitaries. No one else on Gaspar's side of the stage could see back there now, even if they'd been looking.

Which they probably weren't, because the enlarged photographs magnetized attention like flames drew bugs. The portrait that interested Gaspar declared a near-perfect American family. Five Westons gathered around Dad and Christmas tree, dressed in matching holiday plaids. Meredith Weston perched on the chair's arm, her husband's arm around her waist. She looked maybe thirty-five, blonde and tan with typically perfect American teeth suggesting she'd been a well-loved child once. Three children. All resembled their mother. You could tell the teenaged daughter, covered with freckles and hiding braces, would grow into her mother's beauty. Twin boys sporting fresh haircuts and suits that matched dad's were already little men. Fortunately, the boys looked like mom, too. Even back then, Colonel Weston wasn't handsome.

The photos reminded Gaspar of his own family.

Four daughters, and his wife very pregnant with his first son. Gaspar loved his family like crazy. He refused to try to imagine life without them.

Weston's family had ended up dead. How could any father possibly do that? Gaspar had never understood it, even as he knew fathers killed their families every day.

An intent-looking uniformed man was moving toward them along the edge of the audience, his gaze scanning the crowd, but returning to Gaspar and Otto. This would be their contact, an Air Force Office of Special Investigations officer assigned to assist the FBI agents in Weston's arrest after the memorial service ended. Otto spotted him, too, and the three of them stepped away at a safe enough distance from the crowd to talk while maintaining a clear view of the parade ground, as well as the stage and surrounding elements.

"Agents Otto and Gaspar?"

They nodded.

"Did you get what you came for from Weston? We might manage another few minutes before the arrest if you need it."

"Actually—" Otto replied, looking for his name plate.

"Call me Danimal. Everybody does."

"Danimal," she said.

"That's right."

Otto shrugged. "OK, Danimal. I'd like more than just another few minutes with the guy. Two days in a room alone with him, maybe. He knows a lot more than he's telling."

"Sorry. Can't happen," he said. "Happy to spill whatever I know, though. Not that there's much to spill. Reacher was a good cop and he did a good job on the case. He had a good close record on his cases, but he couldn't make it stick against Weston. Everything's in the file. I've read it. We can't release the file, but my boss promised yours that I could answer your questions."

"Not a lot of Army here on base back then, right?" Otto asked. "How was this case Reacher's jurisdiction, anyway?"

"Strictly speaking, it probably wasn't. Weston was on base for a few months on a special assignment. Reacher came down after the murders."

Gaspar asked, "So Reacher wasn't assigned to duty here?"

"No need for Army military police like Reacher. Base security handles everything. In appropriate cases, we coordinate with Tampa P.D. and the local FBI. Sometimes other jurisdictions."

"Weston was Army. What was his assignment?"

"Classified," Danimal said, as if no further comment was necessary.

"Weston lived off base. Why was base security involved in the case?"

"All MacDill security teams have good relationships with local law enforcement. We work together when our personnel are involved."

Otto said, "Reacher disregarded all the standard procedures, I gather."

He nodded. "Murder of an Army officer's family is not the sort of thing we'd keep our noses out of just because it happened off base."

"Weston and Reacher had a history," Gaspar said. "That have anything to do with Reacher's interest?"

Danimal shrugged. "Weston had a history with everybody who crossed his path. He's not an easy guy. You must have noticed."

Gaspar said, "Wife and three kids shot in the head with a .38 while they slept in their own civilian beds around midnight on a Wednesday. Ballistics on the gunshots?"

"It was the wife's gun. First responders found it on the bed still loosely gripped in her hand. Army wives learn to shoot for self-protection and she was damn good at it. In this case, looks like she didn't get the chance to fire."

"Reacher concluded there'd been no intruder?"

"House was in a good, safe South Tampa neighborhood, but shit happens sometimes."

"Not in this case?" Otto asked.

"Right." He nodded. "No forced entry, no identifiable evidence of a break-in. Front door locked and alarm system activated. Family dog asleep in the kitchen."

"The dog slept through the whole thing?" Gaspar asked.

Danimal nodded. "That's what it looked like."

Gaspar had to agree. Dogs don't sleep through break-ins. Not unless they're drugged, or deaf. Or they know the killer. And sometimes, not even then.

"Say Reacher was right. No intruder," Otto said. "Normal conclusion would be murder suicide. Yet the locals ruled that out and Reacher agreed. Why?"

"No motive, for starters."

Gaspar nodded. Women usually need a reason to kill, even if it's a crazy reason.

"By all accounts, she was a wonderful mother, decent wife to a difficult guy. Kids were great, too. Good students. Lots of friends. No substance abuse."

"All-American family, huh?" Otto asked,

glancing again at the photographs on the stage.

Danimal shrugged. "Zero reported difficulties."

Which was not the same thing as no problems, exactly. Gaspar was forming a clearer picture of Reacher's analysis of the crimes. "Suspects?"

"No."

"She have any enemies?"

"None anyone could find."

"How hard did Reacher look?"

Danimal shrugged again. "Not too hard, probably. He knew Weston. We all did. Guy had plenty of enemies. We didn't need to spin our wheels looking for hers."

"Where was Weston at the time of the murders?" Otto asked.

"Alibi was weak from the start," Danimal said. "He claimed he was drinking with buddies at a local strip joint until the place closed."

"Devoted family man that he was. Alibi didn't hold up, though?"

"No confirming surveillance available in those clubs, for obvious reasons. Nobody remembered Weston being there after his buddies left about two a.m."

Gaspar said, "Meaning Reacher focused on the most obvious suspect."

"Pretty much," Danimal said. "Reacher wanted Weston to be guilty, sure. But the rest of us agreed. Reacher wasn't completely wrong."

"Roger that," Gaspar said.

"What happened next?" Otto asked.

Danimal looked uncomfortable for the first time. "That's a little…vague."

"Let me guess," Otto said, sardonically. "Weston was hauled in looking like he'd been run over by a bus, right?"

Danimal shrugged and said nothing.

"What persuaded Reacher to abandon charges against Weston?" Gaspar asked.

Silence again.

Otto asked, "So what happened after Weston's arrest?"

"Case was over, as far as we were concerned. The situation moved up the chain of command, out of Reacher's purview. He returned to his regular post."

"Where was that?"

"Texas, maybe?" Danimal said.

"But that wasn't the end of things, was it?"

"Pretty quickly, local detectives concluded Weston's family had been killed by a cheap hit man."

"How cheap?" Gaspar asked.

"Five-hundred dollars, I think, for all four hits."

"Anybody could have paid that," Otto said. "Even on Army wages."

Danimal didn't argue. "They couldn't tie Weston to the killer, so charges against Weston were dropped. Reacher had no say in the matter. Even if he'd still been on base, the result would have been the same."

Gaspar said, "Reacher had to love that."

Danimal laughed. "Exactly."

Otto tilted her head toward Jess Kimball, who was still sitting with the press off to the opposite side of the stage. "Reporter over there says Weston's family was killed to send him a message. Any truth to that?"

"Probably. But that made him a victim, not a suspect. We couldn't prove anything more," Danimal replied.

"How hard did you try?" Gaspar asked.

"If the evidence was there, Reacher would have found it. He was a good cop and he did a good job on the case."

After thinking a bit, Otto said, "After Weston was released, Reacher kept looking for evidence, didn't he? And he let it be known. He hounded

Weston, figuring he'd crack. Or do something else Reacher could charge him for, right?"

Danimal said nothing.

Otto said, "A few of your guys maybe helped Reacher out with that project."

Danimal still said nothing.

Weston was a scumbag through and through. Reacher wouldn't have let that go. Gaspar wouldn't have, either.

"How'd it end?" Otto asked.

"Weston was arrested frequently. Jaywalking. Spitting on the sidewalk. Whatever," Danimal replied.

"Didn't matter as long as Weston was getting hassled and locked up for something and sporting a few bruises, right?" Otto asked.

He shrugged. "When Weston came up for his next promotion, he got passed over. His CO suggested he'd be better off outside, away from, uh, constant surveillance."

"So Weston retired," Otto said.

"Yes."

"And then what?"

Danimal replied, "And then he got worse."

Gaspar figured Reacher had been counting on that. Reacher had sized Weston up and concluded he was a scumbag. Guys like Weston don't get better with age.

While Danimal was briefing them, Gaspar had been preoccupied with Reacher and not watching Weston closely enough. For Gaspar's assignment, Weston was a source of information and nothing more. After he told them what they needed to know, Weston could stand in front of a firing squad and Gaspar wouldn't have cared. Because he agreed with Reacher. Weston killed his family, one way or another. Weston was not the victim here.

Until he was.

CHAPTER SIX

THE SERVICE CONCLUDED. THE chaplain returned to the microphone and asked everyone to stand and bow their heads. Weston, his wife, and the others on the stage did so, along with the audience. Hushed whispers from the respectful crowd stopped. The only noises Gaspar heard were muffled by distance. The chaplain began his benediction.

A split second later, the first gunshot shattered the quiet. Automatically, Gaspar's gaze jerked toward the sniper nests he'd located—was that a rifle's glint he saw snugged up against that HVAC unit?—then back to the stage. He counted two more rapid shots. Like a crazy break dance, Weston's body lurched forward, propelled by the force of each impact from behind, not from any identified nest. Had Gaspar imagined the rifle's glint?

After the third shot, Weston crumpled like a marionette whose strings were abruptly severed.

When Weston fell, he opened a window for the fourth shot, which hit Samantha Weston.

The fifth bullet struck the chaplain.

Gaspar and Otto were already rushing the stage with their weapons drawn after the third shot, but their sightline behind the stage was still obscured. They'd left Danimal behind with his own weapon drawn, scanning the crowd for the shooter as he got on his radio.

Like a brief time delay on live television, the audience began screaming and chaos erupted just as Otto reached the stage with Gaspar half a step behind. As Gaspar followed her around the left side of the stage, he counted five additional, rapid shots originating from the parking lot behind. Followed by no further shooting.

When they reached the parking lot, two men were down and two more stood over the bodies.

The chaos became choreographed as moves practiced during countless drills were automatically performed almost simultaneously as Danimal's base security took charge.

Weston was approached, triaged, and rushed into one waiting ambulance. Mrs. Weston was rushed to a second ambulance.

The chaplain's injuries were either fatal or minor, judging from the medics' lack of urgency when they reached him.

More security personnel arrived. Two men were confirmed dead.

Within minutes the entire base was locked down. The voice came on the speaker advising everyone to "shelter in place." Meaning hunker down until the situation was secured.

Otto and Gaspar hung back from the working professionals.

"We should go," Otto said, her attention focused on the crime scene. "Those two authorized FBI agents will be around somewhere, maybe calling backup. We can't be caught here."

Though Gaspar agreed, he told her to wait there a minute and slipped around the edges to reach Danimal, who was questioning Weston's bodyguards. The same bodyguards who'd failed to protect their boss. Danimal stepped aside to give Gaspar a brief account of the shooting according to the first witnesses.

"Looks like a lone shooter. That guy," he

pointed to one of the two dead men. "No ID yet. He approached the back of the stage about halfway through the service as if he was authorized to be there. When Weston stood for the benediction, he pulled his pistol and shot Weston in the left shoulder, and both legs. Mrs. Weston was shot in the right femur. The other victim is one of Weston's bodyguards. These two guys say the shooter killed their buddy and then they killed him."

Gaspar reviewed the crime scene briefly, then nodded. "It could have happened that way," he said. "Where did they take Weston?"

"He requested Tampa Southern," Danimal said. "Call me later and I'll fill you in. I've got to get back to work."

"Thanks," Gaspar said, then approached the two bodies for a closer look.

The bodyguard lay face down, lifeless, unmoving in a lake of his own blood. Black hair. Bulky guy. Maybe six feet. Maybe 200 pounds of pumped-up shoulders and biceps. Big, but not big enough to stop bullets fired dead on target at close range.

Less than three feet away, the scrawny shooter was face up on the tarmac, one glassy eye still open and the other covered with a black patch. Like several others attending today's memorial, grotesque scars from a healed wound gouged his forehead. One cheek was sunken because half the upper jawbone had disappeared some time ago. His Army BDUs were well worn and oversized for the wasted body inside them. Boots polished but old and scuffed as if he'd had trouble lifting his feet to walk. His deformed right hand still gripped the FN Five-seven pistol he'd meant to use to get up close and execute his target.

Brain injuries manifested in unpredictable ways. It was possible the shooter had been unable to control his homicidal impulses and simply lashed out at the nearest targets, but the whole scene felt darkly, undeniably intentional to Gaspar. Shooting Weston in the back. Shooter knowing he'd die trying to kill. Hitting Weston three times before the two wild shots injured others nearby. A crowd of military families and personnel watching.

It felt very, very personal.

No question the shooter was a man with vengeance on his mind.

But he wasn't Jack Reacher.

Gaspar wondered if Reacher would experience a pang of regret for having his unfinished business with Weston finished for him by this damaged, deranged soldier.

After he'd absorbed all he could about the situation, Gaspar returned to Otto and said, "Let's go."

They slipped weapons back into place and merged with the audience as security herded them to their cars and eventually exited the base though the nearby Bayshore Gate.

While they waited in the long line of traffic, Gaspar told her about the glinting rifle barrel in the sniper's nest, the bodyguard, and the shooter.

"The shooter's definitely not Reacher?"

"Definitely not. Although it could have been him in the nest. Impossible to know."

Otto nodded, thinking. "So. Disabled veteran? Maybe served under Weston's supervision?"

"Iraq has been Weston's location for long enough. They could have crossed paths there, even if Weston wasn't the guy's CO," Gaspar said. "The shooter was disabled, for sure. Likely a vet. But if we're betting, I'd say he was focused and lucid when he planned and executed this plan."

"Why?"

"Two reasons. First, logistics. Getting close enough to Weston to shoot him required stealth and cleverness, but also logic and planning. He had to get on base, locate the best shooting position, have a weapon, and a long list of other things. None of that could have been accomplished if he'd suffered from a significant mental deficiency."

Otto nodded, considering. "Maybe. One thing we know: the number of vets who suffered head injuries during both Iraq and Afghanistan is staggering. In earlier wars, they wouldn't have survived wounds like that. We can keep so many more alive now, but the treatments aren't great and definitely don't fix the damage."

Gaspar said nothing.

"Sometimes, they suffer strokes and seizures. Behavior can be erratic, even violent," Otto said, running through her internal list of possibles. "Maybe he had a grievance against Weston. And maybe he was just not rational. What's your second thing?"

"He pulled it off. He reached Weston, armed, on a military base designed to stop him. He shot five times before a private bodyguard took him out, but not before he mortally wounded the bodyguard. And he had physical disabilities beyond the head trauma. All of that says logic, planning, knowledge, focus." Gaspar took a deep breath. Discussions about the abilities of the injured and disabled were bound to lead somewhere he wasn't willing to go.

"My money says the guy specifically planned to kill Weston and he was willing to die trying. But with nothing more to go on, it's impossible to know. And, more to the point, not our case. We've got our own problems. So now what?"

"Assuming Weston survives, those two FBI agents will execute his arrest warrant today, no matter what," Otto said. "Let's see if we can get any more out of him about Reacher before we lose the only good lead we've got."

"Okay. But what about Reacher?"

"What about him?"

"If he was the one in that sniper's nest, he knows Weston wasn't dead at the time he got into the ambulance. And he knows where to find Weston now."

"And he's at least thirty minutes ahead of us," Otto said.

Gaspar increased the sedan's speed to tailgate the car in front of them. Maybe today was the day to face Reacher after all. Get some answers right from the source. Finish this assignment and move on.

CHAPTER SEVEN

TAMPA SOUTHERN HOSPITAL WAS located about six miles from MacDill Air Force Base near the opposite end of Bayshore Boulevard. Gaspar stretched out as he settled into the oversized seat and drove along perhaps one of the most beautiful stretches of pavement in Florida.

Immediately outside the Bayshore Gate they passed residential property on the west side of the winding two-lane. At the first traffic light, Interbay Boulevard, more than half the traffic turned west.

Gaspar continued through the residential section, past the streets that led to the Tampa Yacht Club entrances on the right, past Ballast Point. After the next traffic light at Gandy Boulevard, the two lanes separated into a wide divided linear park that ran along the entire shoreline of Hillsborough Bay toward downtown.

Otto seemed to enjoy the scenery, too. As they passed Plant Key Bridge, she said, "I've never been to Tampa before. What's that little island out there?"

"It's called Plant Key. Privately owned. It was originally built by a railroad baron named Henry Plant."

"He built an island?"

"Well, the Army Corps of Engineers dredged the bay and piled up the dirt, but Plant did the rest. That Moorish looking building was his home, called Minaret. Maybe built in the 1890's. Plant was constructing the Tampa Bay Hotel, now the University of Tampa. He was competing with Henry Flagler for the rich and famous vacationers of the time."

"Don't try to tell me about competition, Chico," Otto said. "I'm from Detroit, where the weak are killed and eaten. There've never been rivals bloodthirstier than the Fords and the Dodge brothers."

He laughed. "Now, there's a great restaurant out there called George's Place. If we get a chance, we'll have dinner there. The chef is amazing."

Otto glanced toward him and smiled for the first time today. "You mean we'd eat something that doesn't come out of a ptomaine cart? What a sweet-talker you are."

He felt a grin sneak up on his lips and some of the unrelenting tension released. "Stick with me, Susie Wong. You ain't seen nothin' yet. You've never tried a gold brick sundae, I'll bet."

When she laughed like that, she seemed younger and prettier, Gaspar realized. She was so serious most of the time that he'd never noticed that about her. She was young. She could still have a normal life with a family. He wondered if she ever thought about that.

"The homes along here across from the waterfront are amazing, too. I've stayed in hotels smaller than that one," she said, pointing to an 8,000-square-foot Georgian-style mansion. "Reminds me of a similar stretch along Lake St. Claire. In Grosse Pointe, just outside Detroit. I drive out there on weekends sometimes in the summer. Beautiful."

She sounded homesick. Interesting, Gaspar thought. Until now, she'd never seemed to care that she wasn't on her way back for Thanksgiving.

There was no further landmass in Hillsborough

Bay until they reached the bridge to Florida Key where Tampa Southern Hospital was located. Gaspar merged onto the bridge and crossed the water before entering the driveway between the hospital and the parking garage.

"Drop me off at the entrance and park the car, okay?" Otto said. "I'll find out what's going on and meet you inside."

"You got it, Susie Wong," he replied. She left the car and he watched her sign in at the information desk and head toward the elevators before he drove to the garage alone.

CHAPTER EIGHT

FOUR PEOPLE OCCUPIED THE small waiting room when Gaspar arrived upstairs. Two men he'd never seen before. Two women he recognized. The men sat a few chairs apart and directly across from the wall-mounted television tuned to a football game. If they noticed or cared about his arrival, they didn't betray themselves.

He was relieved to see both women look up when he entered, which meant he hadn't become invisible since they'd seen him last.

Jess Kimball, the *Taboo* reporter, sat closer to the entrance, as if to ensure she'd be the first to pounce when worthy prey arrived. There was something about her that suggested barely contained anger. Given her feelings about Weston, maybe she was annoyed that the shooter had failed. She was intense, which made Gaspar want to know her story. She was young to be so driven. Usually that kind of idealism came from tragedy and betrayal, in Gaspar's experience. Which was what he figured had happened to her. But what?

The other woman was Jennifer Lane, Samantha Weston's lawyer. She sat in the corner across from the entry door where she had a clear view of the entire room and its occupants. Gaspar knew a lot of lawyers, but none that were Velcroed to their clients like this one. What was going on there?

He shrugged. Both women were too young to have known Reacher during the Weston murder investigation, which made them vaguely interesting, but irrelevant to his mission.

He absorbed the rest of the scene in a quick glance. One wall of the waiting room featured large plate glass windows overlooking the water. The opposite wall sported a small opening filled with a sliding frosted glass panel behind which, presumably, someone was working. Otto was probably chatting that someone up now. Which was great, because it meant he didn't have to do it.

Gaspar settled into one of the molded plastic chairs, extended his legs, folded his hands over his flat stomach and closed his eyes. The others might think he was sleeping. If nothing interesting happened within five minutes, he would be.

Three minutes later, Otto came in and sat next to him. "I spoke with the Westons' assigned nurse. His name is Steve Kent. He served at MacDill, so he has the necessary clearances, he said. He was also a Navy medic for a while, and respected Weston's service in Iraq. That's why he requested the duty."

"Since when do you need a security clearance to be a civilian nurse to a retired officer?" Gaspar asked without opening his eyes.

"Probably depends on the officer," Otto said. "Anyway, I told him we had a plane to catch and he said he'd take us in as soon as Weston can answer questions."

"Okay," he replied, closing his eyes again. "Did he say anything else I need to know right now?"

Gaspar heard her sigh and imagined she was rolling her eyes, knowing full well what he was up to. Unlike Gaspar, Otto had never been a soldier. She hadn't developed the habit of resting when she could. She got up and left him to it.

When he checked through his lashes, he saw her pacing the room, stopping now and again to glance out the window at Bayshore Boulevard. On a clear day, Gaspar knew she could have seen Plant Key and George's Place and probably all the way to MacDill at the opposite end of the linear park. Not today. Heavy clouds had moved in, bringing congested air that obscured the sightline. He settled his eyes truly shut.

Gaspar figured even if Reacher was in the vicinity, he couldn't reach Weston as long as Weston was still in surgery. Gaspar might have dropped off for a quick twenty winks, but he heard Otto engage in subdued conversation with one of the women. Probably Kimball. Reporters were chatty by nature. Probably not Lane. Lawyers were notoriously tight-lipped. Trying to talk to Lane would be a waste of time. Whatever Otto found out from whoever she was talking to, she'd tell him eventually. He let his breathing flatten and even out as he felt himself dropping again toward sleep.

He was almost there when the door opened and Gaspar raised his eyelids enough to see a woman dressed in pink surgical scrubs enter. "You're the FBI agents?" she asked.

"That's right," Otto said, directing her to the seat next to Gaspar and leaving Kimball and Lane behind her looking miffed at being excluded.

"I'm Trista Blanke, O.R. Patient Coordinator,"

she said. "I've been told I should give you an update on Mr. and Mrs. Weston. They should both be out of surgery shortly. Mr. Weston's most serious wound was the shot to the back of his shoulder. The bullet traveled through his body, which is better than most alternatives. But it nicked an artery. He lost a lot of blood and the repair surgery lasted a bit longer than it otherwise would have."

"And Mrs. Weston?" Otto asked.

"She was wounded in the right thigh. Again, the bullet traveled through, but it shattered the femur. She should be fine once reconstruction is completed," she said. "They'll be in recovery for an hour or so after the procedures."

"When can we talk to them?" Otto asked.

"When they're out of surgery, you can give it a try. But until the anesthesia wears off, they may not make much sense."

"Thanks," Otto said.

"No problem," she said before she approached Jennifer Lane, likely to deliver the same news. Kimball crowded in to hear.

"We are probably wasting our time," Otto said, quietly.

Gaspar didn't argue. Except for the possibility

of running into Reacher, he figured their time could be much better spent eating. He settled back into his waiting posture and reclosed his eyes, hoping for a quiet five minutes.

When Ms. Blanke had completed her mission and advanced toward the exit, Gaspar heard Otto join her, asking, "Where can I get a cup of coffee?"

Four minutes, forty-five seconds later, the football game ended and the two guys who'd been watching left the room. Gaspar was now alone with the two women. In his bachelor days, he'd have considered that a fringe benefit of the job.

Jessica Kimball spoke first. "Are you planning to arrest both Westons when they come out of recovery?"

"What reason do you have for arresting Samantha Weston?" Jennifer Lane demanded.

Kimball replied, "He's FBI. The Asian woman, too. Why else would they be here?"

"Is that true?" Lane asked.

Gaspar's eyes remained closed and he said nothing. Otto would have bristled at the assumption she was Asian. Oh, sure, she looked like her Vietnamese mother. But she considered herself 100% tall, blonde, sturdy, stubborn German, like her father. Gaspar grinned and said nothing.

Kimball walked over and kicked the sole of his right shoe. Not hard. Just enough to jostle a normal person to attention. But the strike sent painful shock waves up his right leg and into his right side where the muscles had collapsed and the nerves touched things they weren't meant to touch.

"You're not sleeping," Kimball said.

"Checking my eyelids for holes," he replied, willing his pain to settle down. Which never worked. Biofeedback was bunk. Maybe pain was in the brain, but despite his exercise of will, his leg settled into the dull thumping he'd long ago accepted as normal. He opened his eyes, but didn't alter his posture. "What can I do for you, Ms. Kimball?"

"Same thing the FBI has been doing for me for a decade," Kimball said, bitterly. "Nothing."

Lane cut in belligerently. "Do you have an arrest warrant for Samantha Weston? You intend to arrest her while she's incapacitated and unable to understand her rights, Agent Gaspar?"

"Obviously, she understands she has a right to an attorney, since you're here," Gaspar replied without moving. "The only way your presence here makes any sense to me is that she's been expecting us. Which means someone tipped her off. When I find out who did the tipping, you may have yourself another client."

The expression on Lane's face suggested he'd hit the bulls-eye. Most leaks were intentional. If someone had warned Samantha Weston of her impending arrest, the notice was tactical. Which made him wonder briefly, as a matter of professional curiosity, what the local agents were really up to with Weston. If they already had a warrant supported by probable cause for arrest, why did they want his wife?

"Maybe I don't need your client, Ms. Lane. I'm only interested in the original murder investigation," Gaspar said. "What do you know about that?"

"Samantha wasn't living in Tampa back then," Jennifer Lane replied. "Nor was I."

Kimball said, "I've investigated thoroughly for *Taboo*, and I was at the gunman's execution. So I probably know more than she does."

The waiting room door opened again and Otto entered with four cups of black coffee. Everyone took a cup and spent a few moments adding and stirring.

Lane sipped and swallowed before she asked, "Are you thinking today's shooting is somehow about that old case?"

"What do you think?" Gaspar replied.

"I doubt it," Otto said. "Seventeen years is a long time for any normal person to carry a grudge."

Like a woman with personal experience, Kimball said, "Not where your kids are concerned, it isn't."

"Say you're right," Lane said to her. "What do you think is going on here?"

Jennifer Lane looked young and inexperienced. How'd she get a powerhouse client like Weston's wife? Curious situation, at the very least, Gaspar thought again.

Jess Kimball was about the same age as Lane, but she seemed more worldly somehow. As if she'd been through tough times that had aged her and forged her titanium spine. She said, "We need to know how today's shooter is connected to Weston. It wasn't a random shooting, because the guy went right up to Weston and fired only at him. When we get the name of the shooter, I should be able to tell you what's going on."

"What makes you so sure?" Otto asked.

"I do very thorough research, Agent Otto. If Weston's sneezed in the wrong direction, I've found out about it," Kimball said, clearly miffed at the perceived slight to her reporting skills. "Listen: this guy is a miserable human being who's caused nothing but heartache wherever he's gone. This wasn't the first time someone has tried to erase Weston from the planet. He's had more lives than an alley cat already. Sorting through the list of people waiting in line for a chance to kill him will take some time."

Before Otto had a chance to reply, the waiting room door opened again. Every time it happened, Gaspar tensed a bit. Expecting Reacher. But so far, he hadn't materialized.

This time, four people entered ahead of a short, stout man dressed in hospital scrubs. The smallish waiting room was instantly overcrowded.

Gaspar recognized the two FBI agents he'd seen at the memorial service intending to arrest Weston for a laundry list of crimes against the government. Lane and Kimball weren't too far off in their assessment of the FBI's intentions, though they had been led a bit astray regarding the identity of the Bureau's official team for the arrest.

There was an awkward moment while everyone seemed blinded by the unexpected presence of the others before the stout man in scrubs began threading his way through the group on his way to the interior door. One of the agents stopped his progress by pulling out his badge wallet. "I'm Special Agent Edward Crane and this is Special Agent Derek Bartos." Crane, Gaspar thought. He knew—and didn't much like—the man. "We're here to take recorded statements from Thomas Weston and his wife, Samantha Weston." Crane pointed toward one of the other two newcomers, a tall redhead wearing jeans and blazer over a white tee-shirt and a pixie hair cut suitable for a woman ten years younger. "This is Judge Willa Carson and her court reporter, Ms. Natalie Chernow."

Gaspar's right eyebrow shot up. There weren't that many Federal judges in Florida and he'd met most of them several times—the FBI and the federal bench routinely worked cooperatively. Judge Carson's jurisdiction was the Middle District of Florida, though, and Gaspar generally stayed in his own sandbox in the Southern District, so he'd never met her.

But he'd heard stories about the freewheeling Willa Carson, who was said to care less for precedent and statutes than her own version of appropriate justice. Some said Carson's conduct was unjudicial. Others said she was a breath of fresh air. All of which, for a law-and-order man like Gaspar, wasn't usually good news. But he'd mellowed lately on the rule-following. He could hardly fault Judge Carson for doing the same.

The stout man spoke up. "I'm Steven Kent, physician's assistant assigned to both patients. Colonel Weston is out of surgery and stable, though he's too groggy to answer questions yet. He'll be moved in about thirty minutes." His tone was not exactly disrespectful, but he wasn't deferential, either. "Mrs. Weston should be moved by then as well. I'll let you know."

Kent turned smartly like a soldier on parade and left without further comment. Brief silence reigned.

Otto stood and introduced herself and Gaspar to the new arrivals before she said, "There's a coffee pot at the station across the hall. Anybody interested?"

Jennifer Lane held out her empty cup and said, "I'd love another one. Would you mind? I'd come with you, but I need to watch these new guys."

Bad move. She'd insulted the FBI, which raised Otto's hackles along with those of the other agents. Gaspar remained unruffled. Lawyers were always sanctimonious, in his experience. Being a lawyer herself, Otto couldn't very well say so. Gaspar hid his grin as she grudgingly collected Lane's cup.

"I'm fine," Kimball replied.

"Judge Carson? Coffee?" Otto offered.

Carson moved to join her, towering over Otto and glancing back as they headed for the door. "Surely you people can play nice until I get back. If not," she looked Gaspar in the eye, "go ahead and shoot them all."

Gaspar laughed out loud. Yep. Judge Willa Carson might be worth the drive up from Miami on the right case. He'd keep the idea in mind. If he ever got back to his normal job.

CHAPTER NINE

AFTER THE DOOR CLOSED behind Otto and the Judge, Crane said, "Agent Gaspar, can I have a word with you outside, please?"

Gaspar stood, stretched, ignored the pain and forced himself not to limp as he followed Crane into the corridor. When they reached the window at the end of the hallway where they were unlikely to be overheard, Crane asked, "What are you doing here, Gaspar?"

"Enjoying the sunshine."

"Still the same smart ass."

"I think you mentioned that the last time our paths crossed, Crane."

"When I saw you at the memorial, I called in.

Miami doesn't know why you're here. Have you gone rogue, Gaspar?"

"Possibly," he replied.

"If you're connected to Weston, you're going down. Got that?"

Gaspar ignored the threat, which was par for the course with Crane. "Rumor says you've got a warrant in your pocket. Brought along the judge herself, just to cover your bases. The bad news, though: you arrest Weston, you won't need a court reporter. He's not talking to you until he gets a lawyer, and probably not then."

"He's got a lawyer, and he'll talk."

"Lane says she's the wife's lawyer. Not his," Gaspar said.

"Not to me, she didn't." If he jutted his chin any farther, he might fall over from the weight of his fat head.

"You're thinking Weston's going to confess to something? Have you ever talked to the guy? He wouldn't tell you how he takes his coffee unless he had a damn good reason."

"He must have a good reason, then."

Gaspar hadn't considered that Weston would confess. He mulled this over, pushed the idea this way and that, like kneading bread. Couldn't make it work.

"What reason?"

"Don't know. Don't care." Crane sounded like a guy grunting his way through the defensive line. "He's committed about a hundred counts of treason. Murder. Grand larceny. You name it. The guy's a scum-bucket. I get it on the record in front of a Federal judge before he croaks, that's all I care about."

"You think Weston is dying? You're planning a dying declaration?" Gaspar laughed a good two seconds before he controlled himself. "He was winged. Two busted legs and a messed up shoulder. That's it. He's not dying. You're wasting your time."

"Wise up. He's got cancer. He'll be dead by the end of the month. It's his wife he's worried about protecting now. He thinks we'll charge her with his crimes."

"Why would he think that?"

Crane shrugged and made no reply. Which was all the reply Gaspar needed. Crane must have threatened to charge Weston's wife. And Weston must have believed the threat. Nothing else would puff Crane's confidence up so far.

Steven Kent came around the corner and saw them standing at the end of the hallway. "You can come in now," he said, then stuck his head into the waiting room and made the same announcement to the others.

"What about Weston's wife?" Gaspar pressed.

"That's his motivation. He's trying to save her ass," Crane said.

Gaspar wondered whether the wife cared that much about Weston, since she'd filed for divorce. He shrugged. "Will it work?"

"Depends on what he says, doesn't it?" Crane strode away from Gaspar like a man who'd spiked the ball in the end zone.

CHAPTER TEN

THEY CROWDED AROUND WESTON'S hospital bed in a large, open recovery room that had been cleared of all patients except Weston and his wife. She was obviously still out cold, but Weston was at least approaching consciousness—quietly moaning, eyelids fluttering. A blanket covered him from the waist down, obscuring the state of reconstruction done to both legs. His shoulder was bandaged, but not casted. Gaspar guessed the repairs were done on the inside.

Unless he perked up pretty markedly, they weren't going to get much of a statement from him. And even if they did and he said something worthwhile, it wouldn't carry much weight later, given the amount of drugs in his system.

Undeterred, Natalie Chernow, the court reporter, had set up her machine near the head of the bed to be sure she accurately heard and recorded anything he might babble. She also activated a tape recorder. Belt and suspenders, Gaspar supposed.

Judge Carson stood at the foot of the bed, the better to see and hear everything as it happened, should anything happen.

Lane said she would act as Weston's representative for the purpose of the statement so they didn't have to call in another lawyer, which wasn't exactly kosher. But nothing about the situation was normal and it wasn't Gaspar's case, so he wasn't going to object. Even though he'd like to whip that "I told you so" smirk off Crane's face.

Lane stood next to the court reporter, Crane and his crony Bartos stood across the bed from Gaspar and Otto, and Kimball pressed herself into position beside them.

"Wait," Lane said to her. "What the hell are you doing in here?"

"First Amendment and Florida's Sunshine law. Press would be allowed in a courtroom for the statement," Kimball pointed out, "so I can't be excluded just because proceedings are in a hospital."

Lane appealed to Judge Carson, who ruled that Kimball could stay. Gaspar and Otto, too. Carson offered no explanation for her ruling.

Gaspar didn't expect to learn much, especially since Weston had so far only managed the occasional groan, though it made sense to play things out just in case he got chatty. You never knew. It was just barely possible he might cough up a lead on Reacher that he and Otto could follow up later. Mainly they stayed because it would have looked odd to leave at that point.

And then Weston opened his eyes. When he saw Gaspar, his mouth opened in a wide, drugged, silly smile. His pupils were dilated and his speech slurred when he gleefully asked, "Did my guys get him?"

"What?" Otto asked, leaning in.

Weston's voice was weak, whispery, hard to hear. But unmistakably cheerful. "Reacher. Shot me. Did my guys kill him? Is he dead?"

Otto asked, "You lured Reacher to the memorial so your bodyguards could kill him?"

Crane glared at Otto, but she didn't see him. Crane spoke up. "Colonel Weston, the shooter was Michael Vernon. He was killed at the scene. You knew him, right? He served under you in Iraq for two years. Hit by an IED, remember? Two buddies died. Vernon survived. Blamed you for the whole thing, would be my guess."

Weston sank into his pillows and closed his eyes again. His breathing became more ragged. Steven Kent must have noticed something irregular on the monitors because he came into the room and checked the machines.

"Ten minutes. No more," he said to Crane. "Otherwise, he won't survive the night."

"You said his injuries weren't life threatening," Crane said.

Kent stood his ground, "I said normally not life threatening. We need to keep it that way, don't you think?"

Crane didn't like it, but he backed off. Gaspar figured Crane's restraint wouldn't last long.

But it was true that Weston looked bad. When he found out his plan to kill Reacher failed, his fragile strength seemed to evaporate. Gaspar wondered how many times Weston's vendetta against Reacher had failed before. Weston's reach was extensive, inside the government and out. Another possible explanation for Reacher's hiding so far off the grid that not even a bloodhound could find him. At least until Reacher could take care of

Weston or something else got Weston first. Which didn't seem so paranoid right at the moment.

The court reporter announced she was ready.

Judge Carson started the proceedings by opening the record and covering all the legal necessities. She said she'd granted an emergency motion for a recorded statement from Mr. and Mrs. Weston because the FBI represented to her that the statement was essential to an ongoing criminal investigation likely to be harmed if Mr. and Mrs. Weston became incapacitated.

And because Weston's counsel consented.

Jennifer Lane made a short statement about the limited nature of her legal representation and her clients' consent. Observers said nothing.

Finally, Crane began his questions. He could have spent the ten minutes he'd been allotted following up on Weston's plan to kill Reacher, which was the only thing Gaspar was interested in hearing about, but instead his questions focused on Weston's private security company operating in Iraq. Each question was accusatory and belligerent, Gaspar thought. Maybe a little desperate. But it didn't matter. Crane was destined to get nowhere.

Weston had exhausted his available energy on Reacher. Now, he was mostly non-responsive. He grunted a couple of times to signal yes or no. He moaned. He seemed to be almost unconscious. Ms. Chernow's transcript would be mostly a list of questions followed by empty spaces.

After the promised ten minutes, Steven Kent returned to check his patient. "I'm sorry, but that's it. Colonel Weston isn't able to continue."

Crane's annoyance was on full display. "But we're not finished."

Kent replied, "For now you are. You can come back in a couple hours and try again if you want. Or you can call me if you don't want to make an unnecessary trip."

Crane opened his mouth to argue again, but Judge Carson said, "Thank you, Mr. Kent. We'll close the record at this time and resume later this evening or as soon as Colonel Weston is capable."

Crane said, "Let's question Mrs. Weston now, then."

Samantha Weston was in the room's only remaining bed. A curtain separated her bed from her husband's. Kent pulled the curtain back and checked her health indicators. He shook his head. "Mrs. Weston is still sedated. She's not able to communicate at this time, either, I'm afraid."

Crane's mouth was set in a hard line. Gaspar

watched him fight to control his anger. He was a pouter, this guy. Too soft. When he didn't get his way, he was whinier than Gaspar's ten-year-old daughter. The thought made Gaspar smile and Crane glared back as if he might start a fistfight. Gaspar struggled not to laugh. He caught Otto's eye and saw her reaction was the same as his.

Judge Carson saw the lay of the land. She did what judges do. She wrapped it up. "Is there anything else anyone wants to put on the record at this time?"

No one raised anything. She closed the record and everyone left the room except Ms. Chernow, who stayed to pack up her equipment.

In the corridor, Crane seized the initiative again. "Judge, we'd like to continue in two hours. We're worried that these witnesses won't survive the night. If they don't, our case will be irreparably harmed—"

Judge Carson headed him off before he could get too amped up. "Fine. Ms. Chernow exists on nuts and dried fruit she carries in her purse. On that diet, I'd be dead in a week, and I'm hungry. Anyone want to join me for dinner at George's Place? No need to change clothes. We can grab a quick bite in the Sunset Bar."

Because refusing a dinner invitation from the judge on your case wasn't a smart move, everyone officially interested in Weston should have accepted.

But Crane said, "I need to review my file to streamline my questions. I'll just grab something from a vending machine."

Agent Bartos, probably figuring it would be a bad career move to contradict his boss, pulled out his wallet and left for the nearest sandwich.

Jennifer Lane seemed torn by indecision. If she stayed, she could keep an eye on Agents Crane and Bartos, but she'd have to stop watching Gaspar and Otto. Not to mention ticking off the Judge on her case. If she went to dinner, though, Crane and Bartos would remain unsupervised and who knows what mischief they'd get up to without her to restrain them.

Gaspar stifled his smirk and glanced over toward Otto, who pretended to yawn, probably to cover amusement.

"I'm in," Jess Kimball announced.

Otto said, "Me, too." Who knew why? Her motives were usually a mystery to Gaspar.

No mystery at all regarding Gaspar's motivation for accepting Judge Carson's invitation. She'd offered to buy and he was hungry. Simple as that.

CHAPTER ELEVEN

JUDGE CARSON'S MERCEDES CLK convertible zipped along Bayshore Boulevard like a homing pigeon on its return flight. Jessica Kimball's SUV followed. Gaspar brought up the rear in the rented sedan.

George's Place was the only five-star restaurant in South Tampa, as far as Gaspar knew. He'd never eaten at another one. Which might not mean anything. He didn't come to Tampa often and he wasn't a big foodie. A good Cuban sandwich was good enough for him. And any dessert made with guava.

The effortless drive from Tampa Southern to the Plant Key location was as beautiful tonight as it had been earlier in the day. Bayshore Boulevard beribboned the water's edge along the miles in both directions. The full moon and lighted balustrade created a warm, magical picture his daughters always loved.

"How about a quick recap?" Otto asked, as if she were actually giving him an option.

"Sure."

She ticked off her conclusions raising one finger at a time as if they were facts. Which they probably were. "Weston put the word out and staged his attendance at this memorial because he wanted to lure Reacher. He believed Reacher would try to kill him. He made himself a human target. Then his bodyguards would kill Reacher. His purpose was to exact revenge on Reacher."

Gaspar didn't argue. Suicide by cop. Maybe a bit pedestrian for a Machiavelli like Weston, but not a rare motive among those angry and feeling persecuted by law enforcement.

"Weston planned to kill Reacher for sixteen years. Don't you think that's bizarre?" she asked.

"I do." No real reason to argue. Cold revenge and all that. Besides, he was hungry and didn't want to prolong the discussion. He rolled the window down, got a good whiff of the exposed plankton at low tide, and promptly filled the hole with glass again.

Otto's speculation started next.

"The Boss knew of Weston's plan and thought it might work," she said. "He knew Reacher could show up. The memorial was well publicized. Reacher might have learned about it, depending on where the hell he's hiding at the moment. The Boss knew we could get caught in the crossfire."

Gaspar shrugged. "Probably."

"You don't care?" she asked, pugnaciously as usual.

He could feel her anguish, but none of his own. He had no illusions about their Boss. This assignment had almost killed them both more than once already. Why should today be different?

"Doesn't matter whether I care or not, Sunshine."

Her shoulders slumped as her steely defiance melted. "He knew, and sent us in anyway," she said. "That's the worst part."

"It is what it is. You know that. Stop expecting him to change." Gaspar had twenty years to go and no alternative career he could fathom. But Otto was ambitious. She had plans. Options. She should move on before this assignment got her killed or ruined her life, whichever came first. She should have moved on already. But he knew she wouldn't. So he said nothing more.

After a couple of seconds of silence emphasizing Otto's malaise passed between them, she asked, "Did you see Reacher anywhere?"

Gaspar remembered the glint in the sniper's nest, but wagged his head. "Weston's delusional. So's the Boss."

She seemed to feel slightly better when he voiced what amounted to confirmation that Otto hadn't been derelict somehow and missed Reacher when he was right there, larger than life.

Gaspar said, "Our flight's at midnight. We've got maybe four hours left to kill before we're stuck here. We can have a decent dinner, find out what that reporter knows about Reacher, go back to the hospital for Weston's statement, and then head out."

When she didn't reply, he said, "You're such a foodie. I figured you'd be thrilled about our dining experience, Susie Wong. You're in for a treat."

"It's about time you took me to a decent joint, Chico," she replied, a small grin lifting the corners of her lips.

Which was also true. So Gaspar laughed and he felt good when she joined in, for once.

CHAPTER TWELVE

BEFORE THE TRAFFIC LIGHT at the intersection of Bayshore and Gandy Boulevard, Carson's convertible pulled into the left turn lane and stopped briefly before crossing the eastbound traffic lanes to reach the Plant Key Bridge. A simple two-lane track lying flat above the shallow Hillsborough Bay. One way on and one way off the private island. Which was probably both the good news and the bad news, depending on the traffic and whether one was inclined to feel trapped.

Carson rushed into the surprisingly crowded parking lot at the front entrance.

The red brick building fairly twinkled in the gathering dark. Indoor lighting spilled cheerfully through the windows. The rest of the place was bathed by floodlights around the perimeter. Smaller light streams punctuated the darkness and the steel minaret on the roof.

Gaspar lost track of Carson and Kimball while he searched for an open parking space.

"This place is amazing," Otto said.

"What? Doesn't your Michigan house look exactly like that?"

"I thought it looked familiar," she said, which made him feel better. She'd emerged from her mood, at least.

"First time I came here," he said, "I was told the place was built as a private home. Can you imagine living in a place like this? Servants and horses and such, of course."

"Pretty idyllic setting for a restaurant, too," she replied, still taking everything in. "Now I really feel underdressed."

By the time he settled the sedan appropriately, Carson and Kimball must have already entered the building. Gaspar stopped to stretch when he got out of the sedan, like always. He acted like he was just being lazy. But the truth was that if he didn't stretch out his right leg, he'd fall flat on his face when he tried to move.

Otto watched and waited. "Kimball says she

knows everything about the murder of Weston's family. Since Reacher was the investigating officer at the time, she may have some Intel or maybe a couple of leads helpful to us. Let's be sure we don't leave here without it, okay?"

"I'm driving. Can't drink. So I won't have anything better to do," Gaspar said and then set off at as quick a pace as he could manage. But Otto kept up easily. Which was how he judged himself and knew he was moving at glacial speed.

CHAPTER THIRTEEN

KIMBALL WAS WAITING AT the hostess station inside the front entrance. "Judge Carson said she'd be right back and we should look for a booth in the Sunset Bar."

"Lead the way," Gaspar said. He'd been inside the building before, but its old-world charm was no less impressive this time. Spanish influence was heavy, dark, massive, and spacious. He imagined gaslights and servants roaming the halls. Maybe his ancestors had served in such a place in Cuba.

The Sunset Bar was a much more casual eatery than Gaspar expected. A television, booths, a well-stocked bar that hugged the entire side of the room opposite the west-facing windows. Gaspar imagined magnificent sunsets could be enjoyed nightly.

Against all odds, there was one empty booth.
The bad news: it was surrounded by listening
ears and watching eyes. Which meant less
opportunity for intelligence-gathering than Gaspar
had hoped.

Kimball slid across the bench and Gaspar settled
in next to her on the outside so he would have more
room to stretch his right leg unobtrusively. Otto
probably noticed. She noticed everything. She slid
across the bench on the opposite side facing
Kimball and leaving room for Carson opposite
Gaspar.

Kimball leaned in and said quietly, "Those two
guys over there?" She tilted her head to her right,
indicating which ones she meant. "They get around.
I saw them at the memorial service today. I noticed
because they were also at the execution of the killer
of Weston's family. A third guy was with them both
times."

Impressive memory, Gaspar thought. Probably
came in handy for a reporter.

Both men were Weston's age. Latin. Heavy-set.
Casually and expensively dressed. They didn't look
exactly like mobsters, but they weren't ordinary
businessmen having an after work drink, either.

Otto was sitting upright now. In a

conversational tone, she asked, "Do you know who they are?"

"That's one of the things on my list to find out."

"What did the third guy look like?" Gaspar asked, although he suspected he already knew.

"Like he'd been to hell and didn't make it back. What you'd notice about him first was a black eye patch covering an empty eye socket. Scars from a healed head injury." She hesitated a second. "Something wrong with one of his hands, too, but I didn't see it well enough to describe."

"That sounds like the fellow who shot Weston this morning. What did Crane say his name was?" Gaspar searched his memory for the name but before it came up, Otto supplied it.

"Michael Vernon."

Kimball nodded slowly as if she was searching her internal hard drive for data on Vernon and coming up empty. Which Gaspar figured was a ruse of some sort. Surely she'd found a way to get a look at the shooter earlier today. If so, she'd have already made this connection. Not that she owed him anything, but what other information was she holding back?

A waiter appeared at the table with menus and took drink orders. All three ordered coffee. Kimball and Otto ordered black. Gaspar requested *café con leche*, the rich, Cuban coffee heavily laced with heated milk.

"What's the best dinner on the menu?" Otto asked.

"You can't go wrong," the waiter replied. "George's Place has the best chefs in the city. The food here in the Sunset Bar is the same you'd get in the dining room."

Otto said, "What did you have for dinner?"

He grinned. "My favorite is the Thomas Jefferson Roast Beef. Hands down."

"I'll have that," Otto said, handing the menu back.

"I'd add the pear salad with gorgonzola," he said.

"Sold."

"Make it two," Kimball said.

"Three," Gaspar said.

"You got it," the waiter replied, before collecting their menus. "Be right back with the coffee while you wait."

When they were alone again, Kimball said, "Like you, I'm handicapped a bit because I don't know Tampa all that well. We can ask Judge Carson who those guys are. She might know, if they're regulars. Or if she doesn't, she can find out, since her husband owns the place."

Otto's eyes popped open a little wider, but Kimball had been watching her quarry and didn't notice.

Gaspar played white knight for Otto and pupil for Kimball at the same time. "I didn't know Carson's husband owned this restaurant. His name must be George?"

Kimball returned her gaze to Gaspar and Otto and her lips turned up in the most natural grin Gaspar had seen from her yet. She had a pretty face when she wasn't scowling. Which had been rarely so far.

"Let's give the Cuban dude a cigar," she said. "Speaking of which, Willa Carson smokes Cuban cigars. You probably didn't know that, either, did you?"

This time, Gaspar did laugh out loud. The flamboyant Judge Willa Carson was becoming more and more interesting. Too bad he wasn't posted to the FBI's Tampa field office. Sounded like a lot more fun than Miami.

"I'll be sure to ask her if she'd like an after-dinner smoke if we have the time." Cuban cigars were illegal, but the tobacco was now being grown in places like the Dominican Republic. The best ones were hand-rolled, of course, and aged until just the right flavor was to be experienced. Gaspar hadn't enjoyed a quality cigar since he left Miami and he missed them.

He'd have asked more questions, but Otto interrupted the foolishness. "So those two guys and the shooter killed today must be locals. These two must also know Weston. Might have known the Weston family shooter, too, if they got permission to attend his execution."

Kimball said, "Makes sense to me."

"So whatever connection all five men have must relate back in time, at least, to the murder of Weston's family," Otto continued.

If you didn't know her, you'd think she was simply musing out loud. But she'd already reached conclusions and was just polishing them.

Gaspar said nothing.

"Makes sense," Kimball replied. "I can't confirm that, based on my investigation so far, but it's a good working hypothesis and probably true. You're FBI agents. You could ask them. It's illegal to lie to a federal agent."

"You said Weston owed money to a gang that he didn't pay," Otto said. "You said that's why his family was killed."

"Yes."

"What kind of gang? Drugs? Human trafficking?"

Kimball shook her head. "The gang itself was probably involved in all of that. But Weston's vice was gambling. Got in way over his head, as gamblers often do."

"Back then, when Weston's family was murdered, gambling was mostly illegal here except for Greyhound racing," Gaspar supplied for Otto's benefit.

"Dog racing?" Otto said. "There's that much money involved in dog racing?"

"I guess there could be," Kimball said. "But Weston's gambling was the illegal kind. The allegations that Reacher investigated at the time involved pari-mutuel betting."

"OTB," Gaspar explained. "Off track betting. Down in the Miami office, we've got several OTB joints on our constant watch list. It's legal and regulated these days. In Florida, OTB is a money maker for the state. But it's also a cesspool of corruption where a guy with a gambling problem can get into really big trouble."

"Exactly. Weston got in way over his head. He was employed by Uncle Sam in a military job that, well, let's just say it didn't pay a million a year."

"He owed a million bucks?" Gaspar asked.

Kimball nodded. "He had no way to come up with that kind of money. He was a high-profile guy here and the gang decided to make an example of him. They told him to pay up or his family would pay for him. Apparently, he chose option two. Scumbag."

Kimball stopped talking while the waiter delivered the coffee.

When he left, Otto said, "You're saying Reacher discovered all of that and arrested Weston, but the locals couldn't prove any of it? So Weston walked away?"

Gaspar thought that sounded exactly like Reacher's methods. He'd have figured everything out and handled the matter himself. He didn't worry much about whether the courts accepted his proof.

Kimball sipped her coffee and returned Otto's level gaze. "That's how it looks from the file and everything else I've found. Weston didn't pull the trigger, but he didn't do anything to stop the killing, either. Of course he denied all involvement. He had an alibi. The shooter confessed. There was no evidence of Weston's debt. No evidence that the threat had been made by the gang or ignored by Weston. The gang leader certainly didn't come forward."

"No admissible evidence against Weston, so he was released. And Reacher was already gone by the time everything was sorted out."

As Otto completed her sentence, the fourth member of their dinner party arrived and slid into the booth across from Gaspar.

"From Weston's questions at the hospital, I gather your assignment has something to do with Jack Reacher," Carson said as she waved to the waiter to let him know we were all collected. Seeing they were drinking coffee, she ordered *café con leche* for herself and picked up the menu for a quick look. Gaspar figured she had to have it memorized by now. "I met him once when he was here."

"You met who?" Otto asked.

"Who was here?" Kimball asked simultaneously.

Carson decided on dinner, put the menu down, and glanced at Otto and Kimball. "Jack Reacher. He didn't stay long. But I'm told he never does."

The waiter took her order and refilled the coffee. He was even more attentive now that the boss's wife was in the house.

"What was Reacher doing here?" Otto asked, after the waiter left.

Carson settled back into the booth and turned slightly so she was facing everyone. She seemed to make a few quick decisions before she answered. "This is not my case. If it were, I wouldn't be discussing this with you. I'm on call tonight and that's the only reason I agreed to preside over the two sworn statements."

Gaspar figured she was splitting hairs for reasons of her own. But Weston was not his concern and Reacher was. He didn't care about her legal balancing act, but he was impressed with the way she slid around the rules without breaking any.

Otto, ever the lawyer, replied, "Understood." Maybe she felt the same way Gaspar did. "We're doing a routine background check on Reacher for the special personnel task force. Anything you can tell us about him would be helpful."

"I looked into the files today when the FBI asked me to preside over Weston's statement and saw that Reacher was here in the late summer of 1997."

A few months after Weston's family was murdered, Gaspar calculated. Also after the killer was arrested and Weston released. About six months after Reacher left the Army, too. He'd failed to get Weston for the murders the first time. His bulldog tenacity must have pulled him back again for another try after his Army discharge, long after he should have moved on.

"I remembered meeting him. He's not the kind of guy you're likely to forget," Carson said. "Weston ended up in Tampa Southern Hospital almost dead that time, too."

"Which explains why Weston didn't attend the first annual memorial service once he was released from jail after his family was killed. And after that, he's been out of the country," Kimball voiced the thought that had occurred simultaneously to Gaspar.

The food was delivered. Carson and Kimball fell on the meal like feral dogs, but Otto ignored her food, focused on Reacher like a heat-seeking missile. Gaspar felt his stomach growling, but felt he should hold back until Otto tucked.

Carson gestured toward the plates. "We don't have a lot of time. We can talk and eat simultaneously. I've done it for years."

Otto lifted her fork and Gaspar dug in as if he hadn't had a decent meal in weeks. Which hadn't. The food was amazing, even better than he remembered. Exactly the sort of meal his wife loved. The beef was rare and crusted with mango chutney. The Madeira mushroom sauce was light but flavorful. The combination of ripe Bartlett pears, Gorgonzola cheese, candied walnuts and vinaigrette perfectly blended. A dry Cabernet would have made the meal one of his wife's all-time top five. Which meant he couldn't tell her about it. At least, not until he could bring her to experience the meal herself.

"We've never met Reacher," Otto said, barely moving her fork around the ambrosia on her plate. "What's he like?"

"Big. Quiet. No fashion sense at all," Carson laughed. When Otto didn't grin, Carson seemed to consider the question more seriously. Slowly, as if she was uncovering buried artifacts from the depths of memory, she said, "He stood out like a sore thumb, but he exuded confidence like a force field that repelled all challengers. He seemed American, but not American at the same time. In the way that military kids do. Like he held a valid passport but didn't really belong here. He didn't seem to care that he didn't belong. He didn't seem to care about much of anything, actually."

"Was he living in Tampa? Or visiting someone?" Kimball asked. Maybe she was thinking about the gambling situation. Or maybe she thought Reacher was looking for Weston, too.

"He said he was passing through. He asked me where the bus station was. Headed north, I think. Atlanta, maybe?" She wiped the Madeira sauce off her mouth with her napkin and sat back from her plate. "Of course, everywhere in the country is north of here, and most roads lead to Atlanta."

Kimball said, "From what you've described, Reacher doesn't seem like the kind of guy you'd even come into contact with, Judge. Where'd you meet him?"

"Didn't I start with that? Sorry. A fundraiser. We attend dozens of those things. This one was education scholarships for military orphans, I think."

"Where was the event held? At MacDill?"

"Greyhound Lanes," Carson replied. She must have noticed their bewilderment. "Not the bus station or a bowling alley. The dog track."

"Dog racing?"

"Yes. Why?"

"Was Weston there?"

"If he was an officer at MacDill then, he might have attended the fundraiser. Sure. Quite a few military folks were there. It's a big annual event. Very popular. Huge family affair."

Kimball looked toward the two Latin kings across the room. "Anything to do with those guys sitting over there? They look familiar to me, but I can't place them."

Carson turned around to check. "That's Alberto and Franco Vernon. They might have been at the fundraiser. They're not involved with Greyhound Lanes. But they do own a pari-mutuel track a few miles north of here."

"Are they related to Michael Vernon?" Kimball asked, naming the dead man Agent Crane had identified as today's shooter.

Carson set her fork on her plate briefly, composing her reply with care because the question came too close to the case she was handling. "They have a brother named Michael, yes. Theirs is a large local family. Long-time Tampa businesspeople. Significant contributors to the community. Like most large families, some members are more successful than others. But they're protective of their own."

Gaspar received the definite message that no further questions would be entertained about the Vernons. Kimball must have received the same message because she didn't press further. After a few moments, Carson picked up her fork and resumed her meal at a slower pace.

Otto, fixated as ever, asked, "Did Reacher say why he was there? At the fundraiser?"

"If he did, I don't recall. But I'd doubt it. He didn't say much of anything. Not a conversationalist, let's put it that way." Carson glanced at the television mounted on the wall above the bar in the corner. "We're out of time. Let's finish up our food and head back. Agent Crane will report me to the chief judge if we're any later."

The way she grinned made Gaspar feel there was a story there about her relationship with the chief judge she wasn't sharing. Which was too bad. Because it was probably one he'd enjoy.

CHAPTER FOURTEEN

OTTO AND GASPAR ARRIVED at the hospital's main entrance first. They signed in again at the information desk and wandered through the maze of some administrator's idea of organized healthcare. Eventually, they located the OR waiting room where they had agreed to rejoin the others two hours ago. Nightfall came early in November, but the view from the waiting room window was no less appealing, Gaspar noticed. Bright moonlight and illumination along Bayshore Boulevard rendered it more magical than in daylight, not less.

Agents Crane and Bartos were seated with open briefcases on their laps amid candy bar wrappers and empty paper coffee cups.

"Looks like you guys enjoyed a gourmet supper, too," Gaspar said.

Crane just glowered at him.

"Where's Jennifer Lane?" Gaspar asked.

Bartos replied, "Samantha Weston asked for her about five minutes ago. As soon as Judge Carson and the court reporter get here, we'll all go back in there and finish up and get out of here."

As if his words had conjured her, Carson opened the door and said, "Ms. Chernow texted me on our way back. She says she's setting up. Let's get this done so these patients can get some rest."

They all started after her down the hallway toward the recovery room where they had left both Westons.

After less than twenty feet of progress, everything went to hell.

First, the unmistakable sound of two quick gunshots filled the quiet corridor. A woman screamed. Another woman shouted words Gaspar could not make out. And two more quick gunshots followed.

Otto pulled her Sig Sauer and ran forward, ahead of Gaspar.

He pulled his Glock and followed close behind.

Weapons drawn, Crane and Bartos brought up the rear.

Before they reached the room, he heard another gunshot.

Willa Carson ran past them back toward the staircase. An instant later, a horrifically loud buzzing sound exploded around them. She'd pulled the fire alarm. When Gaspar glanced back past the other two agents, he saw the Judge had grabbed her cell phone and was already dialing.

The narrow, hospital-paraphernalia-choked corridor left the agents no choice but to charge single file toward the source of the gunshots.

Just before Otto reached the recovery room doorway, Natalie Chernow dashed out and crashed into her. Otto pushed her against the wall and tried to ask what had happened, but she was sobbing and babbling incomprehensibly. Not that she could've been heard over the alarm in any case, much less over the sirens outside that now joined the cacophony. The din was deafening.

Gaspar supposed he should take comfort in the rapid response rate by everyone involved, but there was no time to appreciate that just then. Otto shoved the court reporter to him and he passed her back to the agents behind him, then followed Otto into the room where he could just hear her shouting "FBI! FBI" over the pandemonium. Sound reverberated through Gaspar's entire body like electroshock.

CHAPTER FIFTEEN

THE FIRST PERSON GASPAR saw was Jennifer Lane.

She stood empty-handed, staring, eyes as wide as basketballs.

The deafening fire alarm continued, now transitioned to incessant blasts brief moments apart, loud enough to wake the morgue.

Just ahead of him, he saw Otto pivot, assume shooter stance and yell, "Hands up! Hands up!"

Steven Kent stood facing Otto, one hand extended with a .38 caliber handgun pointed toward Jennifer Lane.

Slowly, he raised both hands in the air. He pointed the gun in his right hand toward the ceiling.

His blue scrubs, face, arms, and hands were splattered with blood. But he made no further move. He said nothing. He seemed to understand what was expected of a man in his situation and he performed appropriately.

Like the pause button on a video had been pushed, all action stopped for a long moment, and then each actor in the drama flew into perfectly scripted motion.

Agents Crane and Bartos quickly controlled the shooter.

Otto confirmed both Westons were dead.

Gaspar approached Jennifer Lane, who stared as if the scene remained paused at a point when Kent had shot both Westons twice in the head, shot and missed Natalie Chernow, and turned the gun on her.

"Ms. Lane," Gaspar said, grasping her elbow. "Jennifer? It's okay. Are you hurt?" She did not answer. Her face was pale. She was breathing rapidly. Pupils were dilated. The skin of her arm was cold and clammy to his touch.

"Come over here," he said, but the accursed fire alarm continued and he had to shout to be heard. He holstered his weapon and tried to lead her away from the carnage, but her terror acted like adhesive on her soles. She would not move.

Gaspar yelled, "Jennifer! Jennifer!"

Finally, she turned her head to look at him, but she didn't see him. He could tell. Grasping her arm again as gently as he could, he again tried to lead her away. But she wouldn't budge.

She returned her stare toward the bloody mess that had been Samantha Weston.

Gaspar tried once more to get through to her. He shook her a little bit and yelled to be heard over the damned obnoxious buzzing of the fire alarm.

"Jennifer! Let's go!" She didn't move.

Then instantly the fire alarm stopped. Its absence was surreal, and the unnerving quiet acted like a switch to release Jenny from horrified rigidity. Before he could do more than slow her descent with his grip on her elbow, she fainted and collapsed into a pile on the shiny waxed floor.

In the eerie silence, Gaspar could hear Crane repeating the familiar words accompanying arrest, including full Miranda warnings. Bartos had collected Kent's gun and was using his cell phone to call for backup.

Otto asked Kent, "Steven what were you thinking? Why did you do this?"

Kent said nothing, which Kent had the presence of mind to know was absolutely the best thing to do under the circumstances.

Agent Crane led Stephen Kent toward the exit.

CHAPTER SIXTEEN

ON THE INSTRUCTIONS OF one of the other agents, Kimball had been standing inside the recovery room blocking the door to prevent anyone from entering. She moved aside for Crane and Bartos to lead Kent away, then pulled the door closed behind them and approached Gaspar.

"Let's get Jenny into the waiting room. We can talk there."

Gaspar saw Otto making use of the small window of calm before the room crawled with crime scene personnel to capture evidence of the murders with her smart phone. She'd find him when she was finished.

For the first time, Gaspar noticed the citrus scent mingling with the metallic odor of blood and disinfectants.

When he looked again at Jenny Lane's pale face, eyes closed, barely breathing in a heap on the polished floor, Gaspar realized why she'd seemed so familiar. She looked ghostly like the victim in a missing person's case he'd assisted for the Tampa FBI detail with some follow up in Miami. The two could have been sisters, even. That victim had disappeared from her home and he'd never heard what happened to her. But her name wasn't Jennifer Lane.

He shrugged. He'd seen look-a-likes before. But he felt better that he'd finally made the memory connection.

Kimball collected Jenny Lane's things from the chair and helped him lift her from the floor. He couldn't carry her. He could barely support his own weight. But with Kimball's help, they were able to move Lane into the corridor.

Agent Bartos stood guard outside the recovery room to secure the crime scene until appropriate crews arrived. In the corridor, the business of a quiet hospital floor between surgeries was returning to normal as hospital security calmed patients and personnel. Soon, a different sort of chaos would ensue as the crime scene was processed.

Gaspar and Otto would escape before then.

CHAPTER SEVENTEEN

THE OR WAITING ROOM would no doubt become command central for the remainder of the night as the scene was processed. For now, the room was available. Gaspar and Kimball half carried, half walked Lane down the hallway.

Willa Carson stood by the door and allowed them to get Jenny settled inside. Ms. Chernow was there composing herself as well.

"Can I have a word with you?" Kimball asked Gaspar. He followed her to a quiet corner. "You're not supposed to be here, are you? Your work is confidential, isn't it?"

He didn't confirm or deny, but her powers of observation hadn't failed her.

"You and Otto should get out while it's still

possible. I'll stay here with them and if we find out anything else, I can let you know."

She was right. They needed to go. If Otto didn't show up quickly, they'd be stuck here too long answering too many questions in direct contravention of their orders. The Boss wouldn't like it. But more importantly, he might not be able to erase them from the crime scene once official reporting began.

"Why do you think he did it?" Gaspar asked.

"Why did Kent kill both Westons using the same technique the shooter used to kill Weston's family?" Kimball replied. "Or why did Weston offer himself as a human sacrifice to kill Reacher?"

"Both, I guess."

She shrugged. "Who knows?"

"What's your best guess? That's a place to start."

"The first attack on Weston today was pretty straightforward. Weston was a cat with nine lives. Michael Vernon, the poor dead veteran who tried to kill him, had to be a guy Weston screwed over, like Agent Crane said."

"Makes sense."

"From there, though, it gets tangled. Like I told you, Jenny Lane said Samantha had filed for divorce and offered to testify against her husband to save as much as possible of her assets. Probably a ploy to keep herself out of jail, too."

"Did Lane share any of that testimony with you?" Gaspar asked.

"Not yet. Tangle number two: Weston got a death sentence when he was diagnosed with advanced small cell lung cancer a few weeks ago." Gaspar knew of the cancer, but let her talk. It was almost always a good idea to let people talk themselves out. "Untreatable. He was living on borrowed time. If he'd been conscious when they brought him in here this afternoon, he'd probably have refused those surgeries. It's a miracle he survived them."

"What's your theory on Kent? Why the hell would he do it? Weston was loony enough to hire his own hit just in case Reacher failed to kill him."

"Lung cancer is a nasty way to die," Kimball pointed out. "Weston was a soldier. He would have preferred a quick bullet to the head."

"And then he finds out his wife is about to betray him, so he orders up a two-for-one hit?"

Kimball nodded. "I got about that far down that rabbit hole, myself," she said. "But then—"

"What self-respecting hit man would do his

work, then just stand there and let himself be taken into custody?"

Kimball nodded. "Exactly. Not much of a business model. Unless that was part of the deal. Because that's effectively what the first shooter did, too. He left the Weston house, but he was easy to find."

"Or it could have been bad timing. Maybe Kent thought he'd have time to get away and we returned too soon," Gaspar sighed. "Either way, it leaves us nowhere that makes any sense."

"I wish that were true," Kimball said, her mouth had pressed into a grim line. "Because now I'm thinking I dropped the ball."

"How do you figure?"

"I should've remembered."

"Remembered what?"

"Weston's first wife. Meredith Kent Weston. She was Steven Kent's sister."

So it could have gone either way. Vengeance or contract. Gaspar had stopped trying to find logic in criminal behavior long ago. Life wasn't like fiction. Most of the time, he never learned why. Not that it mattered, really. Weston and his wife were just as dead either way.

CHAPTER EIGHTEEN

TAMPA INTERNATIONAL AIRPORT HAD to be one of the easiest airports in the country. Returning the sedan was quick and simple. Security lines were short. For once, they were at the gate without having to run.

Gaspar figured none of this was good news to Otto. She hated flying. The process went better when she didn't have time to change her mind about boarding.

The seats in the gate area were standard black and silver sling seats. Knockoffs of a contemporary design that most normal people had never heard of. All filled with tourists and kids and wrinklies headed in or out of the Sunshine state to avoid winter weather or celebrate Thanksgiving.

Otto seemed unusually preoccupied, even for her. She had her laptop open, her smart phone at her ear. She'd checked in with the Boss. Working. Always working.

She was number one. He was number two. He was only mildly surprised to realize now that he liked it that way.

Gaspar stretched out, folded his hands over his flat stomach, and closed his eyes. He had about thirty minutes to doze. A rare gift.

Otto pushed his arm to wake him up from sweet oblivion ten minutes later.

"What?" he said, not opening his eyes.

"Kimball sent me a file. Take a look," she said.

He glanced over to her laptop screen. Two photos. Each of a brown envelope. One larger than the other.

The larger was hand addressed in block printing to Samantha Weston, c/o Jennifer Lane, Esq. The postmark was Washington, D.C. ten days ago. No return address. Apparently, the large envelope had contained the smaller one.

The smaller envelope looked a little worse for age and wear. Dirty smudges around the edges of a square about the size of a deck of playing cards suggested its contents. Black letters that looked like printing on a police report were placed across the flap to show they were written after the envelope was sealed.

Thomas Weston Recorded Statement
10:04 p.m. 9/1997
The envelope's seal had been broken.

Otto scrolled up the screen to the email from Kimball. The subject line was *Received tonight from J.L.*

Gaspar said, "Kimball said Lane had offered to share Samantha Weston's evidence against her husband. That must be it."

Because Otto would have already noticed, he didn't mention the handwriting on both envelopes looked like Reacher's. They'd seen several examples from his old case files where he printed the same way.

Otto nodded. "Kimball attached an audio file of the contents of the cassette tape in the envelope. I've listened to it. It's a full confession. Definitely from Weston in his own voice. He admits everything Reacher said at the time about how and why Weston's family was killed. And a little bit more."

"Such as?"

"Two big things. He and Samantha were having

an affair at the time of the murders. And Weston knew the gang would kill his family, but he put everything in place and then just let it happen. Like a kid choosing to let his dog sleep in the middle of the road, even though he knows he's bound to get run over. He knew they were going to die. He simply didn't know when."

"So you figure Kent found all of this out somehow and that's why he killed them both today when he had the chance?" Gaspar asked.

"I don't have to figure anything. I know he found out today, because Weston told him. Jennifer Lane was right there."

"Weston's plan to get Reacher was a bit more clever than we realized, I guess. He had a Plan B if the suicide by Reacher didn't work at the memorial service." Gaspar resettled himself in his chair and nodded at Otto to go on.

"Weston was defeated," she said. "But he had one last chance. When they loaded him into the ambulance at MacDill, he asked to be transported to Tampa Southern. And he asked for Steven Kent, too. Kent told me it was because he had the necessary clearances. But like you said, what clearances would he need to care for an ex-officer?"

"Weston asked for Kent because he knew him. I can buy that," Gaspar said.

"All Weston had to do was point Kent and let him fire, and make sure Samantha went down with him. He manipulated Kent by telling him what was on that recorded statement and demanding that Jennifer Lane play it."

Gaspar wasn't sure all of this held water, but most of it was plausible. And he didn't want to spend his next twenty minutes arguing with her. Weston wasn't their case. Never had been.

He closed his eyes again. "Good to know. But I never doubted Reacher's evidence against Weston anyway. Did you?"

"That's not the most interesting part though," she replied.

He felt her place one of her earbuds to his ear and turn up the volume on the recording. "This was on the end of the Weston taped confession."

For the first time, relaxed in the Tampa airport, eyes closed, almost asleep, Gaspar heard Reacher speak. It had to be him.

The voice wasn't what he'd expected. Range was higher, for one thing. Tenor, not bass. Speech clipped. Accent sort of non-descript Midwest American. If Gaspar had been pressed to describe it to another officer, he'd have said Reacher sounded less dangerous than he knew him to be. Maybe that's how he got close to his targets.

The words were about what Gaspar had guessed, though.

Reacher said, "You got lucky, Weston. You ever step out of line again your whole miserable life, I'll find you. And I'll make you sorry. Count on it."

Gaspar felt his lips turn up of their own accord as he wondered whether Kent had pulled the trigger on that .38 this afternoon at all.

THE END

Want to find out how The Hunt for Jack Reacher began?

Read on for an excerpt of

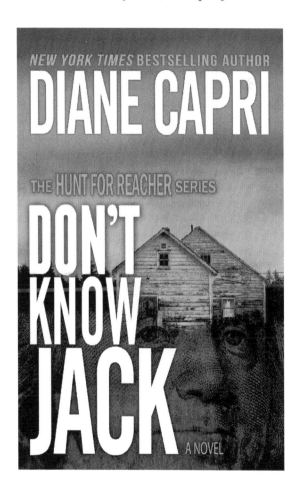

CHAPTER ONE

Monday, November 1
4:00 a.m.
Detroit, Michigan

JUST THE FACTS. AND not many of them, either. Jack Reacher's file was too stale and too thin to be credible. No human could be as invisible as Reacher appeared to be, whether he was currently above the ground or under it. Either the file had been sanitized, or Reacher was the most off-the-grid paranoid Kim Otto had ever heard of.

What had she missed?

At four in the morning the untraceable cell phone had vibrated on her bedside table. She had slept barely a hundred minutes. She cleared her throat, grabbed the phone, flipped it open, swung her legs out of bed, and said, "FBI Special Agent Kim Otto."

The man said, "I'm sorry to call you so early, Otto."

She recognized the voice, even though she hadn't heard it for many years. He was still polite. Still undemanding. He didn't need to be demanding. His every request was always granted. No one thwarted him in any way for any reason. Ever.

She said, "I was awake." She was lying, and she knew he knew it, and she knew he didn't care. He was the boss. And she owed him.

She walked across the bedroom and flipped on the bathroom light. It was harsh. She grimaced at herself in the mirror and splashed cold water on her face. She felt like she'd tossed back a dozen tequila shots last night, and she was glad that she hadn't.

The voice asked, "Can you be at the airport for the 5:30 flight to Atlanta?"

"Of course." Kim answered automatically, and set her mind to making it happen.

Showered, dressed, and seated on a plane in ninety minutes? Easy. Her apartment stood ten blocks from the FBI's Detroit Field Office, where a helicopter waited, ever ready. She picked up her personal cell and began texting the duty pilot to meet her at the helipad in twenty. From the pad to the airport was a quick fifteen. She'd have time to spare.

But as if he could hear her clicking the silent keys, he said, "No helicopter. Keep this under the radar. Until we know what we're dealing with, that is."

The direct order surprised her. Too blunt. No wiggle room. Uncharacteristic. Coming from anyone lower down the food chain, the order might have been illegal, too.

"Of course," Kim said again. "I understand. Under the radar. No problem." She hit the delete button on the half-finished text. He hadn't said undercover.

The FBI operated in the glare of every possible spotlight. Keeping something under the radar added layers of complication. Under the radar meant no official recognition. No help, either. Off the books. She didn't have to hide, but she'd need to be careful what she revealed and to whom. Agents died during operations under the radar. Careers were killed there, too. So Otto heeded her internal warning system and placed herself on security alert, level red. She didn't ask to whom she'd report because she already knew. He wouldn't have called her directly if he intended her to report through normal channels. Instead, she turned her mind to solving the problem at hand.

How could she possibly make a commercial flight scheduled to depart—she glanced at the bedside clock—in eighty-nine minutes? There was no reliable subway or other public transportation in the Motor City. A car was the only option, through traffic and construction. Most days it took ninety minutes door to door, just to reach the airport.

She now had eighty-eight.

And she was still standing naked in her bathroom.

Only one solution. There was a filthy hot sheets motel three blocks away specializing in hourly racks for prostitutes and drug dealers. Her office handled surveillance of terrorists who stopped there after crossing the Canadian border from Windsor. Gunfire was a nightly occurrence. But a line of cabs always stood outside, engines running, because tips there were good. One of those cabs might get her to the flight on time. She shivered.

"Agent Otto?" His tone was calm. "Can you make it? Or do we need to hold the plane?"

She heard her mother's voice deep in her reptile brain: *When there's only one choice, it's the right choice.*

"I'll be out the door in ten minutes," she told him, staring down her anxiety in the mirror.

"Then I'll call you back in eleven."

She waited for dead air. When it came, she grabbed her toothbrush and stepped into shower water pumped directly out of the icy Detroit River. The cold spray warmed her frigid skin.

SEVEN MINUTES LATER—OUT of breath, heart pounding—she was belted into the back seat of a filthy taxi. The driver was an Arab. She told him she'd pay double if they reached the Delta terminal in under an hour.

"Yes, of course, miss," he replied, as if the request was standard for his enterprise, which it probably was.

She cracked the window. Petroleum-heavy air hit her face and entered her lungs and chased away the more noxious odors inside the cab. She patted her sweatsuit pocket to settle the cell phone more comfortably against her hip.

Twenty past four in the morning, Eastern

Daylight Time. Three hours before sunrise. The moon was not bright enough to lighten the blackness, but the street lamps helped. Outbound traffic crawled steadily. Night construction crews would be knocking off in forty minutes. No tie-ups, maybe. God willing.

Before the phone vibrated again three minutes later, she'd twisted her damp black hair into a low chignon, swiped her lashes with mascara and her lips with gloss, dabbed blush on her cheeks, and fastened a black leather watch-band onto her left wrist. She needed another few minutes to finish dressing. Instead, she pulled the cell from her pocket. While she remained inside the cab, she reasoned, he couldn't see she was wearing only a sweatsuit, clogs, and no underwear.

This time, she didn't identify herself when she answered and kept her responses brief. Taxi drivers could be exactly what they seemed, but Kim Otto didn't take unnecessary risks, especially on alert level red.

She took a moment to steady her breathing before she answered calmly, "Yes."

"Agent Otto?" he asked, to be sure, perhaps.

"Yes, sir."

"They'll hold the plane. No boarding pass

required. Flash your badge through security. A TSA officer named Kaminsky is expecting you."

"Yes, sir." She couldn't count the number of laws she'd be breaking. The paperwork alone required to justify boarding a flight in the manner he had just ordered would have buried her for days. Then she smiled. No paperwork this time. The idea lightened her mood. She could grow to like under the radar work.

He said, "You need to be at your destination on time. Not later than eleven thirty this morning. Can you make that happen?"

She thought of everything that could go wrong. The possibilities were endless. They both knew she couldn't avoid them all. Still, she answered, "Yes, sir, of course."

"You have your laptop?"

"Yes, sir, I do." She glanced at the case to confirm once more that she hadn't left it behind when she rushed out of her apartment.

"I've sent you an encrypted file. Scrambled signal. Download it now, before you reach monitored airport communication space."

"Yes, sir."

There was a short pause, and then he said, "Eleven thirty, remember. Don't be late."

She interpreted urgency in his repetition. She said, "Right, sir." She waited for dead air again before she closed the phone and returned it to her pocket. Then she lifted her Bureau computer from the floor and pressed the power switch. It booted up in fourteen seconds, which was one fewer than the government had spent a lot of money to guarantee.

The computer found the secure satellite, and she downloaded the encrypted file. She moved it to a folder misleadingly labeled *Non-work Miscellaneous* and closed the laptop. No time to read now. She noticed her foot tapping on the cab's sticky floor. She couldn't be late. No excuses.

Late for what?

FROM LEE CHILD
THE REACHER REPORT:
March 2nd, 2012

The other big news is Diane Capri—a friend of mine—wrote a book revisiting the events of KILLING FLOOR in Margrave, Georgia. She imagines an FBI team tasked to trace Reacher's current-day whereabouts. They begin by interviewing people who knew him—starting out with Roscoe and Finlay. Check out this review: "Oh heck yes! I am in love with this book. I'm a huge Jack Reacher fan. If you don't know Jack (pun intended!) then get thee to the bookstore/wherever you buy your fix and pick up one of the many Jack Reacher books by Lee Child. Heck, pick up all of them. In particular, read Killing Floor. Then come back and read Don't Know Jack. This story picks up the other from the point of view of Kim and Gaspar, FBI agents assigned to build a file on Jack Reacher. The problem is, as anyone who knows Reacher can attest, he lives completely off the grid. No cell phone, no house, no car...he's not tied down. A pretty daunting task, then, wouldn't you say?

First lines: "Just the facts. And not many of them, either. Jack Reacher's file was too stale and too thin to be credible. No human could be as invisible as Reacher appeared to be, whether he was currently above the ground or under it. Either the file had been sanitized, or Reacher was the most off-the-grid paranoid Kim Otto had ever heard of." Right away, I'm sensing who Kim Otto is and I'm delighted that I know something she doesn't. You see, I DO know Jack. And I know he's not paranoid. Not really. I know why he lives as he does, and I know what kind of man he is. I loved having that over Kim and Gaspar. If you haven't read any Reacher novels, then this will feel like a good, solid story in its own right. If you have...oh if you have, then you, too, will feel like you have a one-up on the FBI. It's a fun feeling!

"Kim and Gaspar are sent to Margrave by a mysterious boss who reminds me of Charlie, in Charlie's Angels. You never see him...you hear him. He never gives them all the facts. So they are left with a big pile of nothing. They end up embroiled in a murder case that seems connected to Reacher somehow, but they can't see how. Suffice to say the efforts to find the murderer, and Reacher, and not lose their own heads in the process, makes for an entertaining read.

"I love the way the author handled the entire story. The pacing is dead on (ok another pun intended), the story is full of twists and turns like a Reacher novel would be, but it's another viewpoint of a Reacher story. It's an outside-in approach to Reacher.

"You might be asking, do they find him? Do they finally meet the infamous Jack Reacher?

"Go...read...now...find out!"

Sounds great, right? Check out "Don't Know Jack," and let me know what you think.

So that's it for now ... again, thanks for reading THE AFFAIR, and I hope you'll like A WANTED MAN just as much in September.

Lee Child

ABOUT THE AUTHOR

Diane Capri is a *New York Times*, *USA Today*, and worldwide bestselling author.

She's a recovering lawyer and snowbird who divides her time between Florida and Michigan. An active member of Mystery Writers of America, Author's Guild, International Thriller Writers, Alliance of Independent Authors, and Sisters in Crime, she loves to hear from readers and is hard at work on her next novel.

Please connect with her online:

Website: http://www.DianeCapri.com
Twitter: http://twitter.com/@DianeCapri
Facebook: http://www.facebook.com/Diane.Capri1
http://www.facebook.com/DianeCapriBooks

If you would like to be kept up to date with infrequent email including release dates for Diane Capri books, free offers, gifts, and general information for members only, please sign up for our Diane Capri Crowd mailing list. We don't want to leave you out! Sign up here:
http://dianecapri.com/contact/

Printed in Great Britain
by Amazon